BURNT TOAST

DEVOTIONS FOR IMPERFECT PEOPLE

JAN HEMBY

Cover Design by Dee Graphic Design
www.deegraphicdesign.com

Published by Blue Ink Press, LLC
Printed in the United States of America
www.blueinkpress.com

ISBN-13: 978-1-948449-00-7
ISBN-10: 1948449005
Library of Congress Control Number: 2017964073

This book is dedicated to my family who loves me despite all the toast I have burned, both literally and figuratively.

CONTENTS

LATE BLOOMER

When authors refer to their editors, you get the sense they've placed these people in the same category as their dentist or an emergency room doctor. People you need, but there's always pain involved in what they do. While I'm the first to admit that a manuscript returned to me full of red ink has reduced me to drawing the curtains, eating undisclosed amounts of chocolate, and watching low-rated Lifetime movies, editors are a necessary part of the publishing process.

I'm grateful that my editor, Amanda, is both a brilliant writer and a dear friend. I look for any opportunity to snatch her away to a local coffee shop, hoping that some of her talent and creativity will rub off on me.

My first book was published a few weeks shy of my fifty-fifth birthday. Following the launch, Amanda and I met on numerous occasions and drank *lots* of coffee, as it was a busy time for both of us. For one such meeting, I had a notation on my calendar that read "review book sales and discuss the progress of the sequel." However, in my head I was thinking,

"Time to meet with Amanda so I can whine, complain, and basically admit I'm too old for this!"

As I pulled into the Starbucks parking lot that day, I wondered if I should patent a type of intravenous coffee delivery system and offer them a cut of the profits. I reflected on how, instead of slowing down with my upcoming birthday, life seemed to be speeding up. When my husband and I had entered the ranks of empty-nesters, I'd envisioned life becoming a leisurely drive through the neighborhood where the speed limit was a calm twenty-five miles per hour. I could handle that. Instead, I felt as though God had deposited me next to Kyle Petty on the starting line of a NASCAR race. The green flag was going down, and I was freaking out.

Beginning a new career or accomplishing a significant goal later in life is traditionally referred to as being a "late bloomer." The older I get, the more I see God's wisdom in creating us to do certain things when we're younger, such as having children. However, sometimes what appears to be a "late bloom" is actually God's plan and timing at work.

I'm learning that God doesn't always go by a formula. You can't put Him in a box. Thus, I'm currently being pried away from what's safe and familiar. Like Sarah in the Old Testament, I'm way past my childbearing years. Yet, God has chosen this time in my life to make me fruitful. As Christians, we believe in the death, burial, and—most importantly—the resurrection of another "late bloomer."

Jesus didn't begin his earthly ministry until he was thirty. In a culture where people married, had children, and died at a much younger age than they do today, this would seem like a late start. I've often wondered why God the Father waited until this time in Jesus's life to lower that green flag. Although, not adhering to the traditions of His day characterized Jesus's ministry from the outset.

When Christ arrived on the scene, He didn't waste any time punching holes into the Pharisees' flawed theology. In addition, he ate with sinners, healed on the Sabbath, and taught about loving your enemies. He didn't fit the image of what they thought the Messiah was going to look like. He was too radical, too unorthodox, and all too willing to expose their hypocrisy. They were looking for a warrior intent on conquering the oppressive rule of the Romans. What they got was a Savior intent on conquering the oppressive rule of sin.

"You see, at just the right time, when we were still powerless, Christ died for the ungodly."

— ROMANS 5:6

The people of Jesus's day understood that they were no match for the Romans. What they didn't understand was that sin held them in an even tighter grip. The law had been given as the standard of righteousness, but it was impossible to keep. This was why a lamb had to be sacrificed. Even that sacrifice was imperfect, and it had to be repeated each year. Jesus was the Lamb of God, the perfect sacrifice for sin, once and for all.

In John's Gospel, Jesus says, "Truly, truly, I say to you, unless a grain of wheat falls into the earth and dies, it remains alone; but if it dies, it bears much fruit" (John 12:24, ESV).

When Jesus shed His blood on the cross, it soaked into the ground as a seed being planted in the dark earth. Sin had brought a curse to the ground. No matter how diligently man toiled, it still produced thorns. The law was similar; no matter how hard we worked to keep it, we always fell short. Jesus's blood was the seed that soaked into the ground to break the curse of the law. He bore the crown of thorns created by sin. After three days buried in a tomb, He rose to life, having defeated sin and death on our behalf.

Jesus is our example for waiting on God's plan and not attempting to jump ahead. His ways are not always our ways. For those of us who feel like late bloomers, we can find peace in the fact that God sees the big picture and that His timing in our lives is always perfect.

PERFECTLY IMPERFECT

I am not—nor have I ever been—photogenic. If you happen to see a good picture of me, understand that where that one came from, there are twenty-five others that were deleted. And that lone photo only happens every so often (I kept the same Facebook profile picture for over ten years). When winter weather causes power outages and the card games get old, there is no better source of entertainment for my family than scrolling through old photos of me. I either have this weird pirate thing going on with my right eye, or my smile looks like someone just put an ice cube down the back of my shirt.

Fully aware that the camera doesn't like me, I cringe whenever someone says those four little words, "Let's take a picture!" So, you can imagine the panic I felt when the editor of our subdivision's magazine notified me that they needed to schedule a photo shoot with me. They were featuring my first book in an upcoming issue and wanted to take some pictures. Immediately I began to fervently pray that the photographer was up to speed on the latest Photoshop techniques. I considered getting one of those cardboard faces that fans hold up at ballgames and gluing Jessica Simpson's picture on it. Or, better yet, renting one of those wooden "your face goes here" displays often featured at the state fair where it's your face and someone else's body. Either of these options would vastly improve my odds at getting a few favorable shots.

We all have physical characteristics that we don't like. A recessive trait in my family is big ears. One of the reasons I delayed getting the short haircut I now sport is because I inherited my dad's ears. I didn't want to walk into the room and have people say, "Oh, Jan's ears just arrived. And look, they brought Jan with them!"

Although my dad drastically overshot with the auditory receptors, he hit the target with noses. Not a proud man by nature, he was quite pleased with his nose. In fact, when I—and then later, my children—brought prospective spouses to meet him, there had to be a type of nose screening. Passing down this ever-so-important facial feature was essential to him, and he didn't want some large or unsightly snout adversely altering the gene pool.

As a career perfectionist, I've spent a lifetime trying to get things as close to perfect as possible. Whether it's correcting the circles under my eyes or bleaching the stains out of the tile grout, there's always something needing my attention. While achieving excellence is a worthwhile pursuit, we all know in our heads when we've crossed the line from excellence to excess. The problem is that perfectionism isn't just a head issue. It's a heart issue too.

I didn't realize this until God began making some changes in my life, uncovering areas that needed tweaking before I moved into the next—and much busier—season. In addition to a few diet and exercise adjustments, He began to put the spotlight on this one thing that consistently causes me to short circuit and burn out.

Perfectionism is tricky because, on the outside, it looks like an "honorable" problem to have. But it imprisons us nonetheless. The good news is that the Truth of God's word sets us free. John chapter 15:4-6 offers a fresh approach to this issue with which many of us struggle. The passage reads, "Abide in me, and I in you. As the branch cannot bear fruit of itself, unless it abides in the vine, neither can you, unless you abide in me. I am the vine; you are the branches. He who abides in me, and I in him, bears much fruit; for without me you can do nothing."

What Jesus is saying to us is that He hasn't called us to be perfect, but to be fruitful. Being fruitful flows out of a close relationship with Him where He empowers and equips us. We become more effective as we allow His joy to be our source of strength. Perfectionism leads to bondage and burnout. Fruitfulness leads to freedom, productivity, and a deep, abiding peace.

Even though I'll never enjoy photo shoots, I don't stress out about them anymore. God made me—squinty right eye, big ears, and all. I may have flaws, but God doesn't make mistakes.

We're all just perfectly imperfect.

THE BARGAIN

For years I've heard people trumpet about deals they've found on Craigslist. Granted, a few may have been fish stories where, instead of the catch getting bigger with each retelling, the price gets lower. (Come on… nobody really gets a front-loading washer and dryer for fifty bucks!) Still, I was intrigued—as well as bit disappointed—since I'd perused the website numerous times without finding anything. Then one day, I struck gold. Or at least really good wood.

As empty nesters, my husband's and my home furnishings consisted largely of the scraps our kids left behind when they moved out. Over the years, we've supplemented with items that, while functional, lacked in quality. That all changed when I found a name brand bedroom suite and dining room suite on Craigslist. According to the ad, the items were in excellent condition. I thought the price was fair, but in keeping with the spirit of buying secondhand merchandise, I submitted a lower, but still reasonable, offer. Much to my delight (at the time) the seller accepted my bid. Savvy shopper that I am, I drove to Chapel Hill where the furniture was located to see it in person before I committed. Once again, I was pleased to see that it was, indeed, as nice as it had looked online.

As I drove back home that day, I was all but declaring a personal boycott on furniture retailers, chiding myself for ever having paid those exorbitant showroom prices. My husband, who is a financial planner, was equally enthused. Then we began the next phase of the purchase: transporting the furniture to our house.

At the end of the process, I totaled up my "savings." True, had I bought this particular brand of furniture (it was solid wood, something we felt in our muscles and joints for days) in a retail store, it would have cost more than what I would have wanted to invest. But here are a few of the expenses we incurred from "bargain" shopping:

1. Rental truck. Don't let that $29.95 price tag fool ya. Much like your cell phone bill, there are miscellaneous charges that get added. Mileage, insurance, gas, and a fee for using their furniture pads and dolly. When I reviewed the bill, I made sure I hadn't been charged for using the air conditioning in the cab.
2. Getting help to move the furniture. One disadvantage of being in our mid-fifties is that none of our peers have all of their original body parts. Prosthetic knees and hips, shoulders that have been sewn back on—this is a depiction of the lineup we have from our age group. So, I found out that the truck rental company has movers that will assist you. (Also not included with the price of the truck.) While this was helpful with loading the furniture, we still had to *unload* it. The movers certainly earned their money, but as the charges

> began to mount, I began to question how much of a "deal" I had gotten.

As my aching back and I were trying to fall asleep the Saturday night after the items were at least on the various floors on which they would reside, I began to have sugar plum visions of that furniture store truck roaring up the street and stopping in front of my house. And then I thought about grace.

> *You see, at just the right time, when we were still powerless, Christ died for the ungodly.*
>
> — ROMANS 5:6

Grace is God doing for us what we can't do for ourselves. No more than I could lift a solid, wooden dresser by myself could I ever bear the weight of my sin. I could work out, exercise, and try as hard as I could, but it would still be too much. The same is true for our salvation. Even our best efforts fall short.

Even though Jesus carried a seventy-five-pound piece of timber up Calvary's hill, it was the weight of our sin that was so crushing. It was the greatest exchange—the best bargain, if you will—in the history of mankind. Jesus, who was sinless, paid full price for our redemption. In return, we receive forgiveness, a fresh start, and the assurance of eternal life.

Now that I'm officially a Craigslist customer, I'll know better next time how to budget for those unexpected moving costs. And when it comes to the burdens and cares of this life, I'll let my Savior do the heavy lifting.

FROM THE DUST

Hello.

My name is Jan. I'm a cleanie. But dust doesn't bother me. While I realize the last part of this admission could disqualify me from being accepted into a higher and more distinguished order of cleanies, it's still true. And it's evidenced by my ability to finger-write my name on any number of surfaces in my home. I'll dust if I'm having company. Otherwise, I rarely think about it.

I also don't like cleaning my oven. My philosophy is that what people can't see, won't gross them out. It's not like it's something that shows up on your driver's license. *"Ma'am I see you're an organ donor, but you haven't cleaned your oven since 1987. Step out of the car, please."*

I only clean my oven if we're moving. For me, a fresh sheet of aluminum foil does the trick until there's a FOR SALE sign in the front yard.

My children are polar opposites in their attitudes toward household chores. By the time she was eight years old, my oldest daughter was making her bed every morning and picking up her clothes. When my youngest daughter came along, I (foolishly) assumed that she would follow in her tidy older sister's footsteps. I soon learned just how different two children from the same womb can be. I tried everything to convert her to a second-generation cleanie. Nothing worked. Even the Barney "Clean Up Song," which converted many a messy youngster into a cheerful picker-upper, had no real impact.

In light of my youngest daughter's propensity toward letting dirty laundry ferment under her bed, I found myself cleaning up for her over the years. This was for my own benefit, as I would rather look at a straightened room than one resembling a breeding ground for biological warfare.

As parents, it's often easier to do things for our children instead of letting them learn by doing it on their own. It never ceases to amaze me how God delegated to His children the responsibility of spreading the message of the Gospel. The greatest story ever told was entrusted to beings created from dust.

Genesis chapter 2 teaches that after God spoke the rest of creation into existence, He formed man from the dust of the ground and breathed life into him.

It's interesting to note that Jesus used dust twice during His earthly ministry. The first is recorded in John chapter 8. This is the account of Jesus writing in the dirt when the Pharisees accused a woman of adultery. It's the familiar passage of "let him who is without sin cast the first stone." The second is recorded in John chapter 9 when Jesus spat in the dirt to make mud to heal a man's blindness.

I think a valuable lesson from both the Old and New Testaments is that dust was just dust until it came into contact with the Creator. It's that breath of life, that touch from the Savior that can take us beyond our human abilities. It's what enables us to love the unloving and forgive the undeserving. It's what empowers us to believe for the impossible. Most importantly, it's what transforms us from a handful of earth to the hands of Heaven.

Not long ago, I moved my living room furniture around. Underneath, I discovered a lot of dust that needed vacuuming. I actually remembered the Barney "Clean Up Song" and tried to keep a good attitude. I guess cleaning the oven should be next on my list.

Emphasis on *should.*

DISTANCES

There are some moms who are reasonable and remain calm when they are unsure of their children's whereabouts. If their teens are a little late getting home from the ballgame, or if they forget to turn on their cell phones after school, these moms don't jump to conclusions. They assume that their youngsters just lost track of time or that there is some other logical explanation.

I've never been one of those moms. To the contrary, the term "Hover Mother" was most likely coined because of me. If my kids were ten minutes late getting home from visiting a friend down the street, I had the police canvassing the neighborhood. In addition, I have the single largest collection of my children's friends' cell phone numbers of any mom I know. At my older daughter's wedding rehearsal dinner, I asked for a show of hands from those I'd called in an attempt to get in touch with my daughter. The room was immediately transformed to look like we were auctioning off a date with a movie star.

As moms, from the time that second line shows up on a pregnancy test, we're connected to our kids. Or, if your children are adopted, it's that first time you see a picture or hold that little one in your arms. By design, as our kids grow, they get further away from us. They go from sleeping in the bassinet next to our bed, to spending the night at Grandma's house, to going to school, to college, and eventually, to marrying and starting families of their own.

When my oldest daughter went off to college, she was only thirty minutes away. There are some who contend that this doesn't really count as "going off to school." However, she did complete a study abroad program in Italy which definitely challenged my hovering tendencies. A few short years later, my youngest daughter chose a college located four hours away. During that transition, if you opened your window on a quiet night, you could probably hear my faith being stretched. Much like labor, it was that ongoing process of releasing my child out into the world. I thought that the worst was behind me. But God wasn't finished with me yet.

I remember when my youngest daughter informed her dad and me that she had elected to do a study abroad program. When she first brought this to our attention, I smiled, thinking, *Okay, I've got this.* I checked my invisible mom uniform and put a little spit shine on that "Study Abroad Survival" badge. But then I made the mistake of asking her where this study would take place. Her reply? *New Zealand.*

My first response was, "So, they no longer offer a study abroad on the *moon*?"

You don't have to have a graduate degree in geography to know that New Zealand is literally as far away as you can get from our home in North Carolina and still be on planet Earth. She went on to present her case for why she wanted to travel to this land that is the last stop before assistance from NASA is required.

I felt like I was in a bad dream where I was falling and

couldn't catch myself. I started thinking of all the things that could go wrong: a plane crash into a rugged mountain with no means of rescue, a rare bug bite that causes her to lose an ear, or even—God forbid—what if the commode water really does flush in the other direction, and she somehow gets sucked into a vortex?

Then the Holy Spirit began to remind me of a very important truth. Psalm 139:7-10 encourages us, "Where can I go from your Spirit? Where can I flee from your presence? If I go up to the heavens, you are there. If I make my bed in the depths, you are there. If I rise on the wings of the dawn, if I settle on the far side of the sea, even there your hand will guide me; your right hand will hold me fast."

While I can't always physically be there for my children, I can release them to their Heavenly Father who can be everywhere they are. And He loves them even more than I do. If I truly believe they are under his protection, then hovering really isn't necessary.

My daughter ended up accepting an internship in the Galapagos Islands. Not as far away, but I still need to figure out how to return this private jet I found on eBay.

DIFFERENT "CULTURES"

When our children were growing up, my husband and I taught them that, compared to the abundance they've always enjoyed, life was harder for us. Otherwise known as "The Baby Boomer Chronicles," these orations were an attempt on our parts to provide our young ones with a good dose of perspective and to help them cultivate hearts of gratitude. However, on those occasions when teenage eye rolls had exceeded their daily limit, they became a form of punishment. In addition to the old standby of "walking to school uphill both ways in the snow," we also emphasized that our cars didn't have air conditioning back then. But the detail sure to bring an audible gasp from our little millennials was when we described having to get up off the sofa to change the channel on the television set.

Another disparity had to do with our diets. My husband and I grew up eating healthy foods such as locally grown fresh vegetables, which were balanced out by our consuming lots of pork, white flour, and soft drinks with all the bad (or good, however you look at it) stuff in them. Today, it's all about whole wheat bread, Greek yogurt, salads, and gluten-free everything. Recently, one of my daughters introduced me to a healthy dietary supplement that frightened me the first time I saw it.

Let me insert here that both of my daughters are excellent cooks. Anyone who knows me would be quick to recognize that this talent was not inherited. Legend has it that my children developed this skill because they had heard that it was possible and wanted to explore unknown territory, sort of like Lewis and Clark. The result has been that whenever they come for a visit, they graciously offer to take over in the kitchen. Of course, I object and insist on doing it myself. My assertion is always followed by an enthusiastic "No!" by everyone within earshot of the kitchen.

However, the day my oldest daughter showed up at my house with a bottle of probiotics, I was horrified. I pointed out to her that there was something swimming around in the bottom of her drink. She seemed unconcerned. So, I repeated my observation, asking her if she wanted me to toss in some fishing line to pull them out. She identified them as "good bacteria" which help your digestive system work well.

Now, as a Baby Boomer, which means I am of a certain age, I know a little something about digestive issues. So, she had my attention.

She went on to explain that these bacteria help us to do, let's just say, that which we may be unable to do on our own. Sort of like Scrubbing Bubbles for the ever-so-important colon. Then it dawned on me. *Grace.*

Grace does for our souls what Probiotics do for our digestive system. Sometimes we truly are incapable of dealing with certain issues. Sin, for example, is something we can't deal with on our own. No matter how hard you try, you will still sin.

However, there's a remedy. Jesus took the sin problem upon Himself. He who was sinless took the punishment for our sins on the cross. God knew we couldn't do it on our own. So, He loved us enough to become the sacrifice Himself. The penalty now dealt with, we have newness of life.

It's like being on trial in a courtroom and being found guilty on all counts. You're on your way to your new home in the slammer when someone steps up and says, "I'll take her place." You're set free while this innocent person, out of his love for you, takes your punishment. Jesus was crucified and Barabbas walked. That's grace.

I eventually tried the probiotic. Without going into a lot of detail, let's just say that those little things swimming in that bottle really know their stuff.

SWEET DREAMS

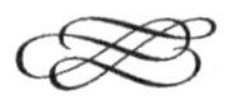

I'm the youngest of three children and, as with most families, was called "the baby" long into my teen years. When we think of the term baby, most of us picture a cute little addition that tags along behind his or her older siblings. While I could be that child at times (back when my red highlights were natural), I could also be a handful.

To be honest, during my waking hours, I was a pretty good kid. It was just when I went to sleep that things started to unravel. My nocturnal shenanigans involved swatting bees in my sleep, running from spiders, and insisting that there were coyotes under my bed. While all of these are strong indicators I should have been medicated as a child, the master of midnight madness at our house was my older brother. He was a sleepwalker, and a legendary one at that. There are many a tale of his wanderings, but two remain staples at the family dinner table to this day.

The first was when his sleep-saturated brain decided that there was never a bad time for a little exercise. He got up, made his exit through the front door, and walked around the house. My parents awoke to the sound of their firstborn knocking on the back door—sound asleep. Another episode, and this is my personal favorite, was when he decided my mom needed a little reading material, again in the middle of the night. She awoke to the sound of his stacking encyclopedias at her bedside. Having become accustomed to living in the house that never sleeps, she assured him that she would get to them in the morning and that he could go back to bed.

Scientists still don't completely understand dreams. There are several theories as to why they occur, including that they stem from something we already had on our mind, something we saw or experienced, or that bratwurst and sauerkraut sandwich we ate before retiring. Dreams can also be given by God, as documented in Scripture.

In Genesis, we read about Joseph, to whom God gave several dreams. His dreams depicted him rising to power and his brothers bowing before him. When he was a younger man, his focus was on how these dreams were about him. Then God allowed circumstances to mature Joseph. He was rejected by his brothers, sold as a slave, and wrongfully imprisoned. When it was time for these dreams to come to pass, Joseph had grown to understand that they weren't about him at all, but were about saving his entire household and all of Egypt from the famine.

Just like Joseph, sometimes God gives us a dream, but it doesn't happen right away. This was true with my first book. God birthed the idea in my heart, but circumstances happened that, from the outside, seemed to be taking me away from it. In reality, God had allowed these pressures to shape and mold me. They served to show me that it wasn't just about me getting a book published. It was about getting the message of God's love to those who needed to hear it.

There are hurting people who can only dream about a life free from depression, addiction, or emotional pain. These don't have to be the kind of dreams that fade when we wake. They are real possibilities that God desires for us. When we surrender to Him, He is willing and able to make them come true.

One bedtime ritual my parents practiced for years was to tell us good night and sweet dreams. After years of bee fights and spider chases, I thought the "sweet dreams" part would never get traction. Now I realize that when God uses us to help those who are lost and hurting, it's a sweet dream indeed.

THE GREATEST OF THESE

There are those who instinctively know how to pick out the right gift. I instinctively don't. My knack for getting it wrong started when I was around eight years old. My older sister and I were browsing through the local dime store when I spotted the most beautiful diamond brooch I'd ever seen. Of course, the brooch contained no real diamonds, or even decent cubic zirconia for that matter. It was an oversized pin garnished with inexpensive pieces of cut glass deposited into a clunky, gold, flower setting. But to my young and untrained eye, it looked like the crown jewels. With a price tag of a buck and a half, I wanted my mom to have it.

So, I bought it, wrapped it up, and proudly presented it to her. I'll never forget the look on her face when she opened it. Part of her reaction was pure joy that her little girl would come up with such a kind gesture. The other part was pure horror at the thought of having to wear this hideous piece of jewelry in public.

But wear it she did. And it was still in her keepsake box when she passed away over forty years later.

By the time I turned ten, I'd matured into a savvy shopper with a keen eye for a bargain. Valentine's Day was approaching and, once again, I wanted to get something nice for my mom. There were decorative boxes of candy arranged in the local drug store display window. One caught my eye. It was heart-shaped and adorned with purple and pink lace. A plastic pink flower graced the center. I really wanted my mom to have it. However, the cost substantially exceeded my weekly allowance. So, I came up with a plan.

Every morning before I left for school, my mom would place a dollar bill on the kitchen table for me. This dollar covered my school lunch and my snack, with a few cents left over. I gave up my snack for several weeks so that I could buy my mom that box of candy. When I had accumulated the necessary funds, I stood on my tiptoes and unloaded a sizable pile of change onto the drug store checkout counter.

Now, let me pause here and say that this purchase set me back about fourteen dollars. That was a lot of money for a box of candy back then, which leaves only one conclusion: this was one BIG box of candy.

As I walked home from the drug store that day, to the casual observer it probably looked like a box of Valentine's Day candy was carrying a little girl and not the other way around. When my mom opened yet another gift from her youngest, she appeared to be thrilled and was proud that I had been so resourceful. As an adult, I remember her chuckling about that big heart-shaped box of candy—a box she kept in the top of her closet for decades.

Sometimes it's hard to find that perfect gift for someone. Valentine's Day is the one occasion when we want our gift to at least come close to hitting the mark, as it focuses on that the virtue that should be our motivation for all giving; and that is love.

In the Bible, there are different words used to define love.

The one that most clearly depicts God's love for us is the Greek word *agape*. Agape is a selfless, sacrificial love; the kind of love that goes the distance. It's what will cause a mom to stay up all night with a sick child, or motivate a dad to work a second job to provide for his family.

The most quoted scripture from the New Testament is John 3:16, and it describes this love.

> *"For God so loved the world that he gave his only begotten son, that whosoever believes in him should not perish but have everlasting life."*

God's love for us was so great that He sent Jesus, who knew no sin, to be the sacrifice for ours. The word *sin* is actually an archery term that means "to miss the mark." The shed blood of Jesus purchased our redemption like an arrow hitting center with unerring precision. When He said, "It is finished," the original Greek translates to "I have done a perfect work, perfectly perfect."

It doesn't get any more perfect than that.

Since this perfect love is a gift, it can't be earned. We don't have to wait until we get our act together or feel like we're deserving of it. We may think our lives resemble the quality of a cheap brooch, but because of God's great love for us, when He looks at us He sees the crown jewels.

I'm grateful that my mom kept those gifts I gave her as a child. She didn't know it at the time, but she was demonstrating how much my Heavenly Father valued me. She and my dad taught me many things for which I am eternally grateful.

But the greatest of these is love.

STRONG COFFEE

I did a word search and discovered that the word "coffee" is mentioned seventeen times in this book. Evidently, I had numerous references in my first book as well. I had friends who, after reading it, told me it made them want a cup of coffee. Not exactly the response I had hoped for. But, with it being my first book, any positive feedback was appreciated!

I come from a long line of coffee drinkers. I didn't become acquainted with that little black bean until midterms in high school necessitated that we meet. In the years that have followed, we've shared countless early morning quiet times and just as many dinnertime desserts.

Of the stories that have spawned over the years by my caffeine-fueled family, this one is my favorite. For decades, my cousin Wesley ran a hardware store just around the corner from Main Street in the town where I grew up. He was a firm believer in "cheaper by the dozen," as was evidenced by every square inch of his establishment being stocked with inventory. His store was not only a place where you could find any sort of gadget you needed (and hundreds that you didn't), but it was also a gathering place for regulars who could grab a cup of hot coffee and catch up on the latest news.

That cup of coffee was an important part of this experience. My dad often told the story of how Wesley's dad, Uncle Fred, took it upon himself to make the coffee from time to time. It remains a mystery to family historians as to whether Uncle Fred was big on water conservation, or simply liked strong coffee. But he would take the leftover coffee from the day before, add a little fresh water to it, and then pour it over fresh grounds.

There were several expressions my dad used to describe this coffee, including one that suggested a transition from boyhood to manhood. At the very least, you were guaranteed to leave the store wider awake than when you entered.

Much like my uncle's eye-opening brew, there are bitter experiences in life that jolt us awake. We get a phone call that a relative has passed away, that same relative we had planned to visit but never got around to it. Or we find ourselves saying that our kids graduated from college a couple of years ago, and then realize it's been six.

> *"Teach us to number our days that we might gain a heart of wisdom."*
>
> — PSALM 90:12

A heart of wisdom alerts us to the reality that life is short. It reminds us that there are certain things we shouldn't put off doing. A heart of wisdom uncovers the hidden wood, hay, and stubble in our lives, exhorting us to spend our time extending God's love and grace to those around us. That load of laundry won't matter a hundred years from now, but the eternal fate of our next-door neighbor will. A wise person will heed the wake-up call and begin putting first things first.

I often think of my Uncle Fred when my morning cup of joe perks up a little stronger than what I'd prefer. I admit there have been times when I've neglected to replenish my stock and had to employ his version of coffee recycling. Perhaps one day, my children will be telling similar stories about me.

At least we're keeping it in the family.

REPLACEMENTS

My mother could make anything grow. She had houseplants that she nurtured for years. If I had a memorial for every houseplant I've killed, the compilation would rival Arlington Cemetery. I'm convinced that the houseplants at Home Depot breathe a collective sigh of relief when I reply to the store clerk that I'm "just looking," as if instinctively knowing that being placed in my shopping cart constitutes an automatic death sentence. Ever the optimist, I remained resolute in my pursuit of a green thumb for many years. But finally, I've had to come to terms with the fact that I am much better at replacing plants than growing them.

Some things in life are fun to replace. For those of us who like to decorate, replacing those dingy throw pillows on the sofa is relatively inexpensive and often improves both your room and your mood. Furniture replacement is even more fun. How memorable was the day when you finally traded in that old, broken recliner—the one that required assistance from the fire department to retrieve your Aunt Edna—for a new one with a cup holder?

And then there are the things that aren't so much fun to

replace. Utility items such as hot water heaters and toilets fall into this category. There are also the dreaded high-ticket items that we all hate to deal with. The pain of these is mostly felt when you write the roofer a check that you're certain could feed a small third world country.

Replacing simply means exchanging one for the other. In Galatians 5:16, Paul instructs us saying, "So I say, let the Holy Spirit guide your lives. Then you won't be doing what your sinful nature craves."

Paul is encouraging us to replace our bad habits with new ones that honor Christ. It's impossible to travel east and west at the same time. If we're seeking to please God and love others, it's difficult to be ungrateful and unforgiving. The result is that our lives, much like a fresh coat of paint to match those new sofa pillows, will bring a touch of His beauty to our surroundings.

By the way, I'm missing a fern that was last seen at the bus station. If you happen to see it, please make sure it finds a good home.

LEFTOVERS

Even though I'm a "cleanie," I'm a sucker for keepsakes. If you walked into my house, you would never know that the same woman who doesn't like clutter—and has a bottle of Windex in each bathroom—also has an attic bulging with memorabilia. With my daughters grown now, I felt it was time to let them take possession of the dance recital costumes, baby blankets, and other remembrances I had saved for them. The impending challenge was obvious: what should I keep, and what should I throw away?

Before I began what I anticipated would be a marathon of box-sorting in the attic, I decided to do a warm up lap in the kitchen. I knew there were dishes and trays I wanted my daughters to have. This would be easy; or so I thought. I began by looking through some stoneware I had received as a wedding present years ago. I climbed onto the counter to reach a rarely used shelf to see what other serving accessories might be stored there. That's when I made a gruesome discovery.

Let me pause here and say that for cleanies, there are certain standards which we try to maintain. While my oven may contain a small landfill of casserole drippings, I do try to keep my pantry in order and generally don't let food expire in the refrigerator. That's why, when I found a leftover cake from Christmas 2014 in my cabinet, I was horrified.

This cake was covered, but as soon as I saw the plastic container, I recognized it. The bakery at the grocery store had featured this cake around the holidays. It was designed to look like a circle of snow-capped Christmas trees. Well, let's just say that the seasons changed during the twelve months this cake spent in my cupboard. Springtime followed winter as those snowcaps had been replaced by a plateful of lush, evergreen mold.

I immediately grabbed my phone and took pictures of this penicillin pastry. I sent it to friends who laughed but also probably made a mental note to never eat dessert at my house again.

Finding this cake was a lesson for me regarding the difference between keepsakes and leftovers. Keepsakes represent memories that you want to preserve. Leftovers represent something that you know you can't keep but aren't ready to let go of yet.

I wonder how many of us have leftover anger, unforgiveness, or bitterness. We know we shouldn't hang on to it, but we aren't quite ready to release it either. What we don't realize is that negative emotions take up space in our hearts and produce all sorts of toxins. We may think we're "managing it" when God wants us to get rid of it. If we took an honest inventory of our hearts, is there a chance we would uncover an attitude comparable to that of a moldy, old Christmas cake? Psalm 119: 11 offers a solution.

"I have hidden your word in my heart that I might not sin against you."

If we have God's word taking up space in our hearts, we won't have room for other things that can hide there. It's impossible for light and darkness to coexist. More importantly, as we allow God's word to transform us into His image, we'll develop His love toward the very people who have hurt or offended us. Unforgiveness imprisons, but God's love empowers. Again, we have a choice: Which do we keep, and which do we throw away?

In addition to finding a decaying cake in my kitchen, I made another interesting discovery that day. Even though the cake was covered in mold, the marshmallows scattered around it for garnishing were perfectly intact. I still have no idea how that cake landed on my cabinet shelf. However, I do know one thing for sure. Marshmallows may not be a nutritious source of food, but they make great, long-lasting keepsakes.

OPEN DOOR

Owning a home is a blessing, but it seems like there is always something that needs to be done to maintain it. From mowing the lawn to changing the furnace filters, the chores never end. One that I enjoy doing from time to time is touch-up painting.

For me, preparing for a painting project almost always involves purchasing new brushes. That's because I'm bad about storing them properly. If you look inside the cabinet in the laundry room where my paint is stored, you'll discover an assortment of cans with brushes half-immersed. You can tell which ones are low in paint, as the lids are fastened. Otherwise, it looks like brushes are trying to either jump in or jump out.

Even though I use water-based paint, I know the rule: adequate ventilation is required. Once when I was painting on a warm spring day, I opened the back door to let in some fresh air. I'm not exaggerating when I say that the door was open for no more than two minutes when a large bee flew inside. I didn't see his illegal entry into my kitchen, as I had walked into the other room. I was alerted to it by that dreaded noise that everyone hates to hear in their house: a buzzing bug making contact with a window pane.

Of course, I was out of insect spray. After a futile attempt of discharging a round of Scotch Guard at him, I stood by the back door. I'm not sure what I was expecting to accomplish, but I did it anyway. In fact, and perhaps this was because of the paint fumes, I began to talk to this bee, trying to coax him out of my kitchen. Even with the fresh, morning air pouring in, he continued to hit against the windowpanes over my kitchen table.

As I stood there cautiously watching this armed intruder, I felt a tug at my heart. Through the windowpanes, the bee could see the outside where he belonged; he just couldn't get to it. This window almost covers an entire wall and, therefore, has lots of panes. He went from one pane to the other, but he couldn't get to the life he could see on the other side.

The solution for this bee was simple: the open door.

When Jesus taught, he used parables—stories from everyday life that people could relate to. As I watched this bee, I felt as if God was teaching me a valuable lesson.

Much like Adam and Eve in the garden, this bee had everything he needed in the environment God had provided for him. I'm not sure what drew him into my house. Perhaps it was a simple navigational error, or perhaps there was something that enticed him. Either way, he became separated from the life for which he had been created. The window, with its numerous panes, reminded me of all the wrong answers and false religions that people turn to. The bee bounced from pane to pane to pane without finding relief or a way out.

Easter is a time when we celebrate Jesus being the Way, the Truth, and the Life. God loved us so much that He took the punishment for all of our navigational errors, wrong choices, and rebellion. The atonement for sin had to come through the shedding of blood. A lamb had to be sacrificed for the sins of the people. Year after year, innocent lamb after innocent lamb. Did you know that when a lamb is about to be slaughtered, it doesn't resist? Jesus didn't resist when He was falsely accused, beaten beyond recognition, spat upon, reviled, and then made to carry a cross beam, weighing at least seventy-five pounds, up a hill.

The Creator became the sacrifice, a King in sheep's clothing.

But it didn't end there. There was a door that was found open that first Easter. It was the door to a tomb, a stone that had been rolled away. The grave was empty. He had risen!

"Where, O death, is your victory? Where, O death, is your sting? The sting of death is sin, and the power of sin is the law. But thanks be to God! He gives us the victory through our Lord Jesus Christ." (1 Cor. 15: 56-57).

Like a bee without a stinger, death and judgement are no longer things we have to fear when we accept the sacrifice Jesus made for us. He took the sting for us. We don't have to keep searching. Scripture teaches us that He stands at the door of our heart and knocks.

We just have to open the door.

ARRIVALS AND DEPARTURES

I'm convinced that, as mothers, we remember things about our children that no one else does. Not that long ago, my daughter flew home to participate in a wedding for a childhood friend. I can recall when she and this friend were only six years old. Sometimes, when I picture the two of them, they still are.

Since my daughter lives out of state now, I picked her up at the airport when she arrived and dropped her back off when her visit was over. At our airport, the location for arrivals and departures is displayed on the same sign, just with arrows pointing in different directions.

I vividly remember the day each of my children were born, and not just because of the hours and hours of intense labor. But rather because of how their entrance into the world caused a drastic change in mine.

For example, before I became a mother, it was my husband's responsibility to kill bugs, spiders, mice, or any other varmint that would attempt to encroach upon our home. My dad had always been the resident exterminator when I was growing up, so I assumed that it was part of the husband/father job description. But, after my children were born, I would have wrestled a bear to the ground if that were what it took to protect either of my little ones.

Sleeping through the night also became a thing of the past —for me, that is. Bottle feedings at 2:00 a.m. were replaced by late night talks with young teenagers needing hearts mended and perspectives restored. And, years later, my cell phone would chirp on my nightstand when a car pulled into a dorm parking lot or when a plane touched down in a foreign country for a study abroad program.

This particular trip for my daughter occurred just before Mother's Day. The afternoon she was scheduled to fly back home after the wedding, we stopped for lunch on our way to the airport. It was here that she gave me my Mother's Day card. The front of it read, "Mom, you taught me to fly." Of course, being a pillar of strength and emotional stability, I cried big, ugly, mascara-running tears and thanked her while blowing my nose on my napkin.

What further tugged at my maternal heart strings happened when I drove her to the airport, following the arrow that directed me to "departures." After she collected her luggage from the trunk of my car, we embraced. Then, unbeknownst to her, she did something that she's done several times throughout her life, each representing a stage of departure. She looked over her shoulder, smiled, and waved.

As I made my way home, my mind went back to years ago when she was in preschool. Each morning I would accompany her up the stairs of the school building where she would continue by herself to her classroom. But before she started down the hallway, she would glance at me over her shoulder and wave. After that, I blinked and it was middle school, high school, college, and then her wedding day. This week she boarded a plane to return to her life in another part of the country, no longer under my care or watchful eye. Her Mother's Day card told me that I was somewhat responsible for her being able to do so; a part of a mom's job description that is both satisfying and bittersweet.

Whether our children are biologically ours or are adopted, they are gifts from God that we get to steward for a just a little while, and then we release them into the world. While our minds accept—and even celebrate—these ongoing changes and adjustments, there is something in a mother's heart that manages to live in more than one time zone. Arrivals and departures exist together on the same sign, just with the arrows pointing in different directions.

When we celebrate Mother's Day, we honor new mothers who have arrived at this milestone for the very first time, as well as mothers (and grandmothers) who have been on the job for decades. We also remember those who have departed, having left their fingerprints on our hearts and lives. Children and mothers will embrace, whether in person, over the phone, or through a treasured memory. The years will melt away as the past and the present collide.

For on this one day each year, time manages to stand still.

PERFECT TIMING

On my first trip to visit my daughter and son-in-law when they lived in Oklahoma, I was preparing myself for two time changes that would be occurring simultaneously: transitioning from Eastern Standard Time to Central Time while adjusting to Daylight Savings Time. Let me go ahead and report that, yes, I was wide awake my first two nights in Oklahoma. However, in an interesting twist, timing became the theme of my visit from start to finish.

For the first leg of my trip, I proudly arrived at the airport ahead of schedule. In fact, I was a little *too* ahead of schedule, as my flight had been delayed forty minutes. That wouldn't have been a problem except that I had a connecting flight in Dallas with only a forty-five-minute layover. I'm not sure how planes can speed, but ours did. (The pilot described it as "making up for lost time.") Still, I had only a few minutes to find my gate in an airport that seemed to swallow me as soon as I stepped off the plane.

I would like to pause here and vent about something that occurs in the airline industry that I'll never understand. The larger the airport, the less information you are provided on your boarding pass. For example, an airport with only two terminals, a vending machine, and a pay phone will issue you a boarding pass with everything but the pilot's cell phone number on it. But at an airport resembling a small city, any information provided is announced by the flight attendant.

So, I'm intently listening for my gate information while calculating how many people I will have to bump out of my way when that ever-so-important seatbelt sign goes off. (Did I mention I was sitting at the back of the plane?) And then the unthinkable happened: they didn't announce my gate. Fortunately, the young lady in the seat beside me pulled up the American Airlines app on her phone and gave me my gate information.

Motivated by the fear of missing my flight, I had no problem asking for directions and double-checking the overhead monitors as I maneuvered along moving walkways and Starbucks customers waiting in line. I finally made it to the airport version of a subway train that eventually spit me out at my gate. With so many people making tight connections, it looked as if Dallas-Fort Worth was hosting a charity run. I heard my name being announced over the intercom as I all but threw my boarding pass at the attendant. Once in my seat, I gave thanks to God for helping me to get there—just in time.

Once at my daughter's home, the time flew by (pun intended). Before I knew it, it was Thursday and I was about to board a plane back home. Once again, my first flight was delayed. Fortunately, I had ample time to make my connection in Dallas. As I was finding my seat, the gentleman sitting next to me offered to help me store my carry-on. We laughed that we had extra legroom—the only perk of sitting right beside the engine. At least we'd be comfortable as we slowly lost our hearing.

Upon talking further—and getting to see pictures of his

lovely wife, children, and grandchildren—it became evident that we both were Christians. He proceeded to tell me that he was in the military and was a short time away from being deployed to Iraq. He was actually looking forward to this assignment, as only a select few had been chosen for it. I thanked him for serving our country and gave him a signed copy of my book, *The Gates Manor Band,* that I had brought with me. It was a small sacrifice on my part compared to the sacrifice that he and his family would be making in the coming weeks and months. We discovered that my book launched on his and his wife's wedding anniversary.

I was humbled at how he felt honored to be sitting next to an author. I was the one who was honored, as I was sitting next to a hero.

Before the Dramamine kicked in and I fell asleep, he shared with me how he wanted God to use him in Iraq to be an example of Christ to the men on his team. I encouraged him that I believed God would do just that. He explained that, originally, he and his men weren't supposed to be on this flight. Due to cancellations and delays, their schedule had been changed. I marveled at how God had remained in control. This was one connection He made sure I wouldn't miss.

Psalm 3:5-6 teaches us to "Trust in the Lord with all your heart and lean not on your own understanding; in all your ways submit to him, and he will make your paths straight."

Sometimes when things don't seem to be working out the way we planned, it is God ordering our steps in accordance with His plan. We can be at peace knowing that, ultimately, He is the pilot.

And His timing is always perfect.

CANCELLATIONS

I don't know why I continue to be so naïve as to expect airline flights to run on schedule. On my second trip to Oklahoma to visit my daughter and son-in-law, my departing flight was delayed again, making my connection in Dallas-Fort Worth another race against the clock. When this happened on my first trip out there, it was merely challenging. The second time, though, it was next to impossible.

As the plane touched down, I began to mentally prepare myself for sprinting through the airport. I quickly collected my carry-on luggage from the overhead compartment and was like a horse snorting at the gate. I decided to check my phone one last time before employing the expression "excuse me" at least thirty times in order to exit the plane. I had one text message, and it was from my daughter.

Your connecting flight has been canceled due to the weather.

Since I had just heard the pilot report that the skies were crystal clear deep in the heart of Texas, I assumed that this was a mistake on her part. I rushed into the terminal to check the arrivals and departures. Sure enough, my short flight from Dallas to Lawton had been canceled. Evidently those big Texas stars make for a wicked glare on late-night departures.

Still not convinced, I waited in line to speak with an American Airlines agent. She clicked the keys on her computer and then announced that she had good news. Even though my 10:05 p.m. flight had been cancelled, they had me booked on another one. There was just one teeny, little problem. It didn't leave until 4:30 the next afternoon.

Now, for those who know me, besides discovering a spider in my bed, this is my worst nightmare. I don't know how to aptly communicate just how bad I am at directions and navigating anywhere outside a ten-mile radius of my neighborhood. I still get lost in downtown Raleigh. At places I've been before. While using a GPS.

I called my daughter, who immediately said her husband would drive to Dallas to pick me up. I understood that he was being very gracious to offer to do that. But I also understood that an underlying motive existed. It was easier to drive six hours round trip to pick me up than to spend days with a search party scouring the vast Texas landscape for my remains.

Suppressing the urge to cry, panic, and otherwise throttle the nitwit who couldn't read a weather forecast, I decided to stay calm. I prayed for wisdom and began to consider my options.

1. Spend the night in the Dallas-Fort Worth Airport. That one didn't stay on the list very long.
2. Get a hotel room in Dallas. Reasoning that I could have flown first class for what a hotel room would cost, that wasn't going to work either.

3. Rent a car and drive to Lawton.

Number three was the winner. I found a rental car company whose contract included a free GPS. The young man who assisted me even typed in my destination address. I made the three-hour drive, arriving safely around 2:00 a.m. But on my way there, something interesting happened.

When I left Dallas, the sky was clear. In fact, it was clear for most of my drive. But the closer I got to Oklahoma, the more I noticed the wind picking up. In the distance, I could see flashes of lightning. As I crossed over into Lawton, raindrops were hitting my windshield. By the time I arrived at my daughter's house, a full-blown storm was raging outside.

None of us like it when our plans get canceled or rerouted. Perhaps your son or daughter didn't get into the college he or she had hoped to attend. Maybe that business deal you worked on for months fell through. You finally got a date with that guy at work only to get a last minute call that he couldn't make it. Or, worse, that girl you planned to marry suddenly changed her mind.

As Christians, we know that there are times when God says no. We never like it, and we often don't understand it. From our limited perspective, it simply may not make sense. The sky looks clear and the path looks bright from where we stand. But our Heavenly Father sees what we may not be able to see—at least not yet. In the distance, there may be a deadly storm that could rip through our lives, leaving our sails torn and our hearts broken. His way may not always be clear in the beginning, but as we trust the roadways—as well as the roadblocks—He allows in our lives, we will see his faithfulness every time.

One of my favorite Scriptures is Jeremiah 29:11, which says, "For I know the plans I have for you," declares the Lord, "plans to prosper you and not to harm you, plans to give you a hope and a future."

We don't have to understand how to fly a plane to trust the pilot. How much more can we rest in the wisdom of our loving Heavenly Father who knows the plans that He has for each one of us. If we let Him navigate, we'll not only reach our destination, but we'll arrive right on time.

HEART PEEL

While I don't believe in evolution, my scaly feet do make me wonder if one of my ancestors had a fling with an iguana. All kidding aside, I have the toughest feet of anyone you'll ever meet. When I get a pedicure, the dead skin that is scraped off resembles a small snow drift. The salon where I get my pedicures done is staffed by Vietnamese technicians. I don't speak Vietnamese, but some types of communication are universal. The way they grimace when I walk through the door leads me to believe they're not exactly happy to see me. Then there's the huddle that follows where a coin toss appears to be taking place. But what really tells me that I'm anything but their favorite customer is when the unfortunate employee who gets stuck with what amounts to thirty minutes of chiseling concrete repeatedly gestures towards my feet and grumbles.

Recently, a friend of mine introduced me to a product she thought could help remove my picture from the dartboard in the nail salon break room. It's a foot peel that can be administered at home. This product contains potent fruit acids that come in two plastic bags, one for each foot. You slip your feet into these plastic bags and let them soak for an hour. Afterward, you wash off the solution and wait for the results, which show up four to five days later.

After this period of time, most people experience an exfoliation that immediately exposes that baby soft skin underneath. However, for me, the process was a bit more complicated. First of all, I knew those fruit acids had their work cut out for them. I wasn't convinced they could completely soak through the bottoms of my feet, which are similar in appearance and texture to an old leather wallet.

Much to my delight, my size six soles began to peel right on schedule. But the peeling was so extensive that it was more like an insect shedding its exoskeleton. For example, I pulled off one piece of skin so large that it maintained the exact shape of my left heel.

Later, as I was changing the vacuum cleaner bag full of foot debris, I realized something. We all have situations that come into our lives that serve to, shall we say, scrape off that top layer of dead skin from our hearts. We may be doing all the right things to keep our hearts healthy, like Bible study, time in prayer, and fellowship with other Christians. All of these disciplines are necessary and beneficial. But even these will have limited impact if our hearts aren't tender and able to receive life-changing seeds.

When Jesus told the parable of the sower in Matthew chapter 13, one type of soil He referenced was the rocky soil. The seed planted in the rocky soil germinated, but the roots never penetrated. So, the plant withered as quickly as it had sprung up. Even when we have the best Bible teachings at our disposal, if our hearts are crusty, then the life-giving instruction will only sit on the surface and produce minimal change. The word itself still contains truth and blessing, but we won't experience the full effect that was intended.

Difficult situations are often allowed in our lives to cut

through the dead traditions, complacency, and other wax build-ups that can form and make us dull. If we allow tough times to do their job, we can be more receptive to all that God wants to in us and through us.

My new goal is to be able to wear a cute pair of sandals I found on sale that are a little too small. One more of those foot treatments should do the trick.

ZONING ORDINANCE

I really, really like my comfort zone. It's where I feel like I can manage my life and, for the most part, control what happens. However, it is becoming clear that God doesn't want my comfort zone to be my permanent address. I can check into it from time to time, much like an overnight stay at a nice hotel, but then it's back to a daily walk of surrender and trust. I know there isn't a scripture that literally says, "Thou shalt not live within thy comfort zone." However, there is one that basically communicates the same message:

"Do not fear, for I am with you."

— ISAIAH 41:10

One area of my life where this applies is the releasing of my two daughters into the plan God—not Mom—has for them. From the time my children left the womb, I've worried about them. I'd panic if they didn't answer their cell phone right away. A missed curfew was grounds for involving the FBI. I'd always hoped they would graduate from college and then have marriages and careers that landed them within a fifty-mile radius of their father and me.

That didn't happen.

When my oldest daughter, her husband, and my two grand-puppies moved from North Carolina to Oklahoma, it felt far away. But far away hadn't happened yet. My son-in-law's next assignment required they move from the sunny Midwest to the land of the midnight sun: Anchorage, Alaska.

If you have even a loose grasp on geography, you'll quickly recognize that Alaska doesn't fall within a fifty-mile radius of the continental United States, much less my neighborhood. To make matters worse, I hadn't even finished sweeping up the South American sand my youngest daughter tracked in from her summer internship in the Galapagos Islands when she began discussing plans to stay with her sister for a short stint following college graduation.

In addition to watching my children's frequent flyer miles accumulate at an alarming rate, I was also being stretched with the ongoing promotion of my book. One such opportunity was my first television interview. It was only a local eastern North Carolina station, but evidently my nerves didn't know this. Even though I had prepared myself for every possible question I could be asked, I was still terrified. I imagined my every word and move being caught on camera. Thoughts that kept me awake in the days leading up to my small screen debut included, but were not limited to:

1. What if my mind went blank?
2. What if I inadvertently distributed airborne spittle when I pronounced hard consonants?
3. What if digestive functions (particularly those that

> are embarrassing and increasingly difficult to govern as we age) decide to upstage me?

Always the optimist, as the day of my interview approached, I regularly watched weather forecasts in the hopes that a lightning strike from thunderstorm might knock out the power. Or, perhaps someone would call in sick. This twisted form of positive thinking kept me going until I pulled up in front of the studio that Monday morning knowing, for sure, that the show would go on.

Of course, my interview slot happened to follow that of a U.S. Senator. I pictured viewers channel surfing and commenting, "Hey, look! Senator Jones is speaking today. Who's that weird spitting lady featured after him?"

But when I sat down in front of the microphone, I was reminded of a truth. Not only was God with me, He was *for* me. I realized that my success wasn't dependent on my skills as a writer or as a speaker. The interview may have been focused on me, but it ultimately wasn't *about* me. I'd been given the opportunity to disclose an eternal truth that was told in story form throughout the pages of my book. Following the Senator's interview, I was able to offer something sure and steadfast that people could secure their anchor to during these troubled and uncertain times: a God who is with them, for them, and—most importantly—loves them.

I'm happy to report that the interview went well and nothing embarrassing happened. In addition, I had the privilege of signing a book for both my interviewer and the Senator. Afterwards, I checked back into my comfort zone for a time of movies and Italian food with my daughter. My Heavenly Father's zoning ordinance went back into effect the next day.

The adventure we all crave exists in a place zoned as

"faith." Biblical faith is based on the eternal and unchanging truth of God and His word. A life lived within our comfort zones restricts us to our limited vision and abilities. A walk of faith launches us into the realm of God's infinite resources.

And with Him at the helm of our lives, anything is possible.

OUTGROWN

Second only to cleaning my oven, organizing my attic ranks as the job I will put off doing for as long as possible. After multiple warnings from my husband that even the strongest floor can only hold so much weight, I decided it was time. So, with a cup of coffee and trash bags in hand, I ascended the pull-down stairs.

It's funny how you can have something in storage for so long that you forget it even exists. Such was the case with the Beanie Babies and California Raisins figures I found. Upon discovering a sizable inventory of dance recital costumes and cotillion dresses, I considered opening a small store. Then there were the Barbie dolls. My oldest daughter loved them as a child. I forgot just how much. Removing the lid from the large bucket containing her collection was a bit eerie, like I was peering into a Mattel mass grave.

But what really captured my attention, and my heart, were the baby clothes. Of course, we had given away most of them over the years, but I did save a couple of boxes. The phrase "they grow up so fast" is never more heartfelt than when you're looking at a toddler-sized Easter dress once donned by your now twenty-two-year-old daughter.

As a mom or dad, it's bittersweet to look through old keepsakes. We're reminded of how time has a way of replacing bedtime stories with curfews, and frilly hair bows are set aside for graduation hats and wedding veils.

Over the years, I've prayed that my children would fulfill the plan and destiny that God has for their lives. As I watched my daughter prepare for her move across the globe, I wondered if I should have prayed harder about them staying in the same time zone as their father and me. I think I was mostly sad that my little girl was no longer a little girl. Then the Holy Spirit gently spoke one word to me:

Outgrown.

I realized in that moment that my daughter had outgrown this past season of her life. It no longer "fit" her anymore. It wouldn't make sense for me to hold her back any more than it would for me to attempt to squeeze her into that toddler dress she wore so many years ago.

Then I thought about the resurrection. After three days, the tomb could not contain the Son of God. Jesus shed the burial wrappings like a garment He no longer needed. Life had replaced death. He had risen!

In the same way, perhaps we need to get rid of things in our lives that are hindering our progress. Much like grave clothes, they're keeping us bound to the past. Maybe it's fear, doubt, or unforgiveness. Whatever it is, it's preventing us from fully experiencing the resurrection life that Jesus purchased for us.

Spring is the time of year where we freshen our wardrobes. We replace bulky sweaters and heavy coats with lighter fabrics and brighter colors. Scripture offers us timeless fashion advice for whatever season we find ourselves in. In Colossians 3:12 we're instructed, "Therefore, as God's chosen people, holy and dearly loved, clothe yourselves with compassion, kindness, humility, gentleness and patience."

These are qualities that never go out of style. Instead of outgrowing them, we grow into them. Best of all, something miraculous happens when you wear this clothing line.

You begin to resemble its Creator.

KEEPING IT CLEAN

My husband loves pillaging the refrigerator. I think he views it as a sacred mission to keep it as cleaned out as possible. To the casual observer, this may seem innocent enough, and even ecologically responsible. However, living with Mr. "No-Leftover-Left-Behind" has its downside.

For example, he's been known to confiscate an entire slab of lunchmeat, meant to be portioned out for school lunches over a week, and pack it with the food he's taking to work. Some years ago, it escalated to the point where our children resorted to labeling their food. The skull and crossbones symbol was the common indicator of which items were off-limits to their dad. In extreme cases, the food went into a type of Witness Protection Program, where we would store the fruit salad designated for the sports awards banquet in a container disguised to look like outdated hamburger.

While my husband's behavior has incited some, shall we say, "lively" conversations around our house, the alternative would be worse. There is nothing more stomach-turning than to uncover a bowl of broccoli and cauliflower that expired during the Reagan administration. Or the disappointment felt when the last container of yogurt has turned into a block of provolone.

It's equally important that we maintain a vigilant watch on our hearts. Proverbs 4:23 instructs us:

> *"Guard your heart above all else, for everything you do flows from it."*

We should keep our hearts free of contaminated inventory such as unforgiveness and bitterness. We don't want people to open the doors to our lives and experience the likes of bad potato salad. Paul also encourages us in 2 Corinthians 2:14, saying, "Now thanks be to God, who always leads us in triumph in Christ, and reveals through us the sweet aroma of his knowledge in every place."

When people begin to see what's inside of us, let's make sure it's life-giving. The knowledge of Christ is both aromatic and satisfying, sort of like that last piece of Mom's pumpkin pie.

Just make sure you grab it before my husband gets home.

ONLY YOU

My brother and sister are eight and six years older than me, respectively. Aside from those occasions when they strictly adhered to the "How to Terrorize Your Younger Sister" manual and tortured, threatened, and otherwise scared the living daylights out of me, I secretly thought it was cool to have older siblings.

One of the perks of being the youngest was having another generation of music to listen to. Before I became a teenager and was playing my own 45s on the family stereo, I cut my teeth on my brother's 8-track collection. I was humming along to The Mamas and the Papas long before The Jackson Five and Elton John became favorites of my contemporaries.

I was especially fond of the love songs of my siblings' generation. One that was quite popular was titled, "Only You." The star-struck crooner of this slow-dance classic told his special someone that she was the only one who could make the darkness light, the world seem right, and other romantic turns-of-phrase that sold over a million records.

As a child, there was another version of "Only You" that I listened to. But it was anything but a love song.

From the time I was a toddler, I've suffered from a dry skin condition. I realize it sounds trivial, and there certainly are worse things to deal with. However, it was severe enough that by the time I started school, I dreaded warmer weather because it meant I would have to wear short-sleeved shirts and shorts. Back then, there wasn't an effective treatment for it. So I was teased and asked why I had bumps all over my skin, and otherwise made to feel like I was different.

I wish I could go back in time and tell my younger self that everybody has something to overcome, even those who seem to have it all together.

One character in the Bible who seemed to have it all together was Elijah. He was a powerful prophet who had seen God do the miraculous. But it only took one bully, a lady named Jezebel, to cause him to lose his confidence. Not only did he run away in fear, but he also retreated to a cave and hid.

When the Lord asked him what he was doing, 1 Kings 19:10 records his response. He said, "I have been very zealous for the Lord God Almighty. The Israelites have rejected your covenant, torn down your altars, and put your prophets to death with the sword. I am the only one left, and now they are trying to kill me too."

One of the devil's oldest tricks is to make you feel like you are the only one. It's "only you" struggling with that addiction. Or it's "only you" trying to live an upright life and not follow the crowd. His goal in making you feel like the odd man out is to isolate you. In doing so, you're more susceptible to succumbing to temptation and discouragement.

The truth is that life brings trials and challenges to all of us. When God responded to Elijah, he assured him that he was not alone, but that seven thousand men just like him were still standing strong. Later, in 2 Kings 6, we read where God encourages another prophet and his servant by allowing them to see the entire army of heaven poised to do battle on their behalf.

The good news is that Jesus, Himself, has promised to never leave you or forsake you. In fact, He still would have gone to the cross even if the person needing His sacrifice was "only you."

IT'S THE LITTLE THINGS

We all have little things we don't like. They are things that, in the big scheme of things, don't really matter. But they bother us nonetheless. Here is a quick list of my top five:

1. Spiders: I could list spiders more than once. I really, really hate spiders. They just look diabolical. And they have too many legs. Nobody needs that many legs. I'm glad they contribute to society by eating insects. But beyond that, they are the stuff of horror movies and nightmares.
2. Fitted Sheets: I have gotten into more than one tussle with a fitted sheet as I've attempted to fold it and put it away. And they routinely pucker on the ends of the bed. If you're not a detailed person, you wouldn't even notice. But they drive me crazy.
3. That unidentified watery substance that squirts out of the mustard or ketchup container on the first squeeze: No comment necessary here. It's just nasty.

4. Lanes that end for no apparent reason: You're driving down the road and then, all of a sudden, you run out of lane. What happened to my lane? And, more importantly, *why*?
5. Dishwasher Scum: That mysterious algae-looking film that occasionally forms on your dishes after they have been "washed" in the dishwasher.

We all have little things that bother us or get on our nerves. Your children's dirty clothes that seem to have a magnetic attraction to the floor but repel landing in the hamper. The time-tested genetic predisposition in men that causes them to leave the toilet seat up. The way your hair will fall perfectly into place on a day when you're planning a trip to Walmart, but on the night of your high school reunion, you can't get it right to save your life.

I believe God uses little irritants as powerful teachers. When I'm ready to sentence that annoying fitted sheet to a life of hard time as a drop cloth, I can remember that I have a nice bed to sleep in. When dirty clothes litter the floor, I can be thankful that these are signs of life from children with whom I've been greatly blessed. When I forget to shake the mustard container before liberally applying it on my ham sandwich, I am reminded that I have a refrigerator full of food.

In 1 Thessalonians 5:18, Paul instructs us to "Give thanks in all things. For this is the will of God in Christ Jesus concerning you." Cultivating a thankful heart enables us to see the goodness of God in all situations. It's the little things that are with us daily that serve as a practice range for us to trust God and develop a posture of gratitude. And when we encounter the big trials, we are conditioned to run with perseverance and peace.

Regarding spiders, I am thankful that I can go to Walmart

with my great-looking hair and purchase a large can of bug spray.

SEVENTH INNING STRETCH

If you're a baseball fan, then you're familiar with the seventh-inning stretch. It's that time when the announcer instructs everyone to stand up, stretch, and sing "Take Me Out to the Ballgame" to the organ music blaring over the public-address system. Beginning each October, this time-honored tradition is recognized at major league baseball's championship event of the year, the World Series.

Besides affording muscular and vascular benefits to those who actually may have been sitting down for seven innings, I wonder if the seventh-inning stretch has another purpose. The late baseball legend Yogi Berra coined a phrase that I think might provide the answer: "Baseball is 90% mental. The other half is physical."

Despite Yogi's glaring lack of mathematical aptitude, I think his logic applies to the seventh-inning stretch. The physical part is the standing up which improves circulation, and helps you discover that there are several pieces of stale popcorn in your seat. Then there's the mental component, which is the singing of "Take Me Out to the Ballgame."

If your team is winning, your excitement and optimism

overshadow the fact that the guy sitting behind you dripped hot dog chili down the back of your jacket. But if your team has no hits and no runs, you might be tempted to pack up your acute case of heartburn and go home. Then you're asked to sing a song about going to a ballgame, and you're reminded of the big picture.

Life's struggles can be that way. Sometimes we get tired of waiting for our team to score. We grow weary of painful situations that never seem to get better. We don't know if we can deal with that illness or broken relationship one more inning, much less into overtime.

The apostle Paul reminds us in Galatians 6:9, "Let us not become weary in doing good, for at the proper time we will reap a harvest if we do not give up." Just when we want to throw in the towel, God reminds us that it's the bottom of the seventh, and, therefore, our faith is being stretched. We have exhausted all of the start-up energy and have entered the phase where it takes something more. If we give up, we won't benefit from the growth, maturity, and perseverance that these situations are designed to build in us. He encourages us to not lose heart.

If we quit when things get tough, we might miss out on a home run that's right around the corner. After all, if it's the bottom of the seventh that means there are still two innings left. And to quote Yogi Berra once again, "The game isn't over until it's over!"

LAWN MOWER LESSON

My parents believed in making us kids work. In addition to pulling weeds in the vegetable garden each summer, we were expected to help out with chores around the house. My signature job was cleaning the one bathroom we had, which included putting a spit-shine to the old brass spigot handles. This was something I took great pride in as a child. In fact, I became indignant if anyone dared to dart in the door once I had everything sparkling clean. I would sternly order any bathroom-seeker to use the woods behind our house. To my knowledge, no one ever took me up on it, but it bought me a little time where I could admire my handiwork a few minutes longer. My family recognized early on that I was a cleanie. As the youngest, I was rarely taken seriously. But when I said, "Don't mess up my clean bathroom," my family knew I meant business.

As a teen, earning my keep extended to the yard when my dad taught me how to use the push mower. Years later, when I had my own children, they became efficient at domestic duties such as cooking, vacuuming, dusting, and doing the laundry. But my husband and I neglected to teach them how to use that ever-so-essential piece of lawn care equipment. This lack of mower know-how was never more evident than the time my oldest daughter decided to cut the grass when her husband, a captain in the army at the time, was away on training for a month.

My son-in-law had stored their push mower in the garage with the handle collapsed. To operate the mower, the handle had to be lifted up and pulled over to the front side.

My daughter didn't know this.

After figuring out how to start it, she began cutting their front yard. The parallel-to-the-ground handle was making what should have been an easy task a back-breaking ordeal. Knowing her husband was taller than she was, she began to feel bad for how he must strain his muscles each week in an effort to keep their lawn looking nice.

She paused for a moment to stretch when she noticed one of her neighbors watching her. The woman called out, "I think you've got that backwards." My daughter smiled and replied, "No, this is how my husband does it."

The neighbor appeared a bit confused, but didn't say anything further. My daughter took note that this neighbor, along with a few others, had stopped what they were doing and were staring at her. I'd like to be able to say that this was a one-time thing. But it wasn't. She cut the grass three times that month while her husband was away. And all three times she did it the wrong—and hard—way.

As I was reflecting on this, I began to think of how, as Christians, the world is watching us. They're observing how we live. Sometimes we do things a certain way because we think it's the right way. Perhaps it's the way our parents did it, or the way our denomination does it. Perhaps it is simply tradition. But it doesn't mean it's the best way. Or, more importantly, that it's God's way.

Grace is a prime example of something that's often "done the wrong way." Biblical grace is defined as us receiving from God the good that we don't deserve. We don't deserve forgiveness, eternal life, or a restored relationship with Him. We're sinners. We only deserve judgement. But God, in His great love for us, extended grace when Jesus took the punishment of our sins upon Himself. This isn't something we can earn.

And yet, as Christians, we often feel as though we can, or that we should. We rely on our good deeds or church attendance thinking that, surely, grace alone isn't sufficient. But scripture assures us that it is.

> *"For it is by grace you have been saved, through faith—and this is not from yourselves, it is the gift of God—not by works, so that no one can boast."*
>
> — EPHESIANS 2:8-9

A Christian who is under grace and still thinks he or she has to earn God's favor is like my daughter not knowing how to properly operate a push mower. She didn't have to work as hard as she did. Plus, if she had put the handle in the correct position, she could have benefited from the power of the self-propel feature.

Accepting the fact that we can't earn our salvation and allowing God's power to work through us is something the world will stop and watch. They'll wonder how we have peace in the face of trials and tragedies. They'll see our love for one another crossing the lines of race, social status, and other labels that divide us. They'll see something at work in our life that's greater than we are. And that something is grace.

Our family still laughs about my daughter's lawn mower experience—a lot. She'll never live it down. My son-in-law now stores the mower with the handle upright.

Just in case.

A FRESH COAT OF SNOW

As a snow enthusiast, I could hardly control my excitement when I scheduled my first trip to Alaska to visit my daughter and son-in-law. I was looking forward to seeing the picturesque, winter wonderland scenery in the land of the midnight sun.

I did see a wonderland. For about three hours. Then it warmed up and rained. I was like a kid expecting to get a toy for Christmas, only to open the gift and discover that it's underwear.

In addition to being disappointed, I was also a bit concerned. I was afraid that I was the carrier of the age-old Southern curse of "whenever it gets cloudy in the winter-time, it warms up and rains." After all, I was in Alaska, where it snows up to an average of seventy-four inches each winter. *Alaska,* where the temps had been in the single digits and below. This phenomenon of forty degrees and raining upon my arrival definitely had me spooked. The locals, on the other hand, were dancing in the streets wearing t-shirts and sandals. (I'm only slightly exaggerating).

Snow is peculiar in that people have strong opinions

about it. You rarely meet someone who says, "I don't really care if it snows or not." They either love it, or they hate it. For Southerners, snow is a tease. It flirts with us from time to time, causing us to spend winter evenings streetlight-staring as we wait for those precious flakes to fall. The grocery store runs are part of the cultural experience started by our ancestors of the twentieth century. Modern Southerners are aware that it's an overreaction and, in most cases, completely unnecessary. We don't really know why we feel compelled to deplete grocery stores of milk, bread, and eggs. Like a dog circling his bed several times before lying down, it's just something that's in our DNA.

Another problem with forty degrees and raining in Alaska is that the snow that is piled up (and trust me, it's *piled up*) on the sides of the road starts turning to slush. This once undefiled thing of beauty becomes soiled with road grime, gravel, and mud. We all know there's nothing pretty about dirty snow. It made me sad to see the changeover.

Then my son-in-law gave me some encouraging news. He assured me that in Alaska, a warm-up is a sign that it's going to snow again soon. I wasn't sure if he was just trying to make me feel better. Perhaps it was false hope. But since he'd been living here and I hadn't, I took his word for it. Sure enough, a day later the white stuff fell again, about eight inches of it.

This event reminded me of grace. Warm ups in life are inevitable. It's those days or seasons where our ice-solid convictions are tested in the heat of the day. We feel our faith melting under the sunlamp of seemingly impossible situations. Bad attitudes and unbelief are exposed. And just when we feel like giving up, grace shows up: that amazing grace that purchased our redemption in the first place. We're reminded that we can't earn our salvation any more than we can make snow fall from the heavens. When the mirror of

God's word reveals our road grime, gravel, and mud, grace covers it once again like a fresh coat of snow.

Romans 5:20 teaches us that "God's law was given so that all people could see how sinful they were. But as people sinned more and more, God's wonderful grace became more abundant."

The more we need grace, the more it is extended. But just as snow needs certain weather conditions to form, grace has conditions as well. It's offered to those who are weak, hurting, and, in some cases, have totally messed up their lives. It's for those who feel rejected, unworthy, and lost.

It's for those who need their sins to be made as white as snow.

It snowed another time during my visit there. The weather when I arrived back in North Carolina? You guessed it. Warm and rainy.

CHANGING SEASONS

I love the idea (emphasis on *idea*) of summer. I envision romantic nights with gentle, warm breezes blowing through the trees. Flowers are at their height of bloom, and the morning work commute is punctuated by the sound of sprinklers watering green, well-kept lawns. Children have more daylight hours to play outside and dot the neighborhood with lemonade stands.

All of this may be true where you live. But where I live, it's miserably hot and humid. On one occasion, I'm almost certain I heard my begonias gasping for air. The Weather Channel tells outright lies about rain so we won't completely lose heart. I wake up each day during the summer to my phone app showing a cloud with a lightning bolt descending, indicating an encouraging forecast of thunderstorms. But, by noon, the cloud has been replaced with a bright yellow sunshine that looks like it's laughing at me. I realize it isn't, but here again, it's probably just the heat.

Fall, on the other hand, delivers the goods. It doesn't just tease us with the possibility of changing leaves and football Saturdays. It comes through on its promises of cooler temperatures and colorful landscapes. Less humidity makes for crisp mornings that are a welcome relief following summer's brutal assault on our sweat glands.

But whether you favor the crack of a baseball bat hitting a pop fly over second, or the music of a marching band at kickoff, we all have our favorite seasons. Ecclesiastes chapter 3 teaches us that life also has seasons. This familiar passage begins with, "To everything there is a season and a time for every purpose under heaven."

The list is extensive, but it includes the following: A time to be born, and a time to die. A time to weep, and a time to laugh. A time to mourn, and a time to dance. A time to cast away stones, and a time to gather stones together. A time to embrace, and a time to refrain from embracing.

It's only natural to look forward to the times of celebrating, laughing, and dancing. But, as this passage instructs, life delivers a variety of experiences, such as seasons of difficulty and suffering. It would be great if we could skip over these. Unfortunately, they are required courses. Some produce pain that, at times, can seem almost unbearable. It could be a situation we're going through personally, or one that's affecting someone close to us. Either way, we've all witnessed trials that could pack a powerful punch.

So, how do we endure summer's oppressive heat of financial distress, or wake up to another day of feeling snowed-in with loneliness following the loss of a loved one? Verse 11 of this passage provides the answer.

"He has made everything beautiful in its time."

Difficult seasons are always served up with a side of purpose. This purpose is to develop strength and perseverance in our lives. These times teach us to have faith when we don't have all the answers yet. We learn how to stand on the unchanging truth of God's word that assures us of His presence and ultimate victory in our lives. There is no situation too complicated and no mountain too big. For with our God, nothing is impossible.

Most importantly, our Heavenly Father uses our trials to conform us into the image of His Son. And that truly is a beautiful thing.

BEGGAR'S BLESSING

We've all driven past the guy on the street corner holding up a cardboard sign. Sometimes we're reluctant to give because we don't know if the person is truly impoverished, or is a scam artist. Or, if you're like me, maybe you don't have any cash on hand in the first place. (Just a note to anyone who would ever consider mugging me: I seldom carry around more than $2.43 in spare change. If you're thinking about taking my credit cards, think again. They're usually maxed out, so that's not going to help you either. In short, robbing me would be both frustrating and unprofitable.)

Something happened to me one Saturday morning that had to do with a gentleman holding up one of these cardboard signs. I was running errands, and my last stop was Walmart. Since it was a Saturday, and I enjoy neither long lines nor the sound of crying children, I decided that the toilet paper we had at home could last another day or so.

As I was driving past the shopping area, I noticed a man standing out in the rain with a cardboard sign that read "AT LEAST SMILE." My mind immediately went to the words of another man in a similar situation who had recently been interviewed by a local newspaper. He recounted having been spit on, cursed at, and humiliated for asking for help. Something about this man's sign tugged at my heart. His message was simple: If you can't help me, that's okay. Just don't make this harder than it already is.

After discovering I had only thirty-seven cents and an old piece of gum in my car console, I went to the ATM to get some cash. When I came back, I could see that this man was genuinely someone in need. He was thin, his face was weathered, and he had lost most of his teeth. I offered a warm "God bless you" with my gift, to which he replied in all sincerity, "Thank you so much. God bless you."

As I drove off, I wondered what he would do with the money. Perhaps he would use it towards a jacket or a warm meal. Perhaps he had a home somewhere in the area. Or perhaps his place of refuge was the inside of a bottle.

Regardless of what I had just given him, he had given me a blessing. This man, whose socioeconomic station had landed him on a strip of earth between a stop sign and a parking lot, had offered me a blessing. Bankrupt financially, but rich in kindness, he gave me the only thing he had in abundance.

Gratitude.

I hope that my small donation helped this man in some way. But I think I was the one who received the greater gift. I was blessed by a man who Jesus would have hung out with. A man who, more than money, wanted someone to smile at him and not further deprive him of his dignity.

In Matthew 25:31-46, Jesus instructs us that when we feed the hungry, give the thirsty something to drink, and visit those in prison, it's as if we're doing it unto Him. Hebrews 13:2 also reminds us, "Do not forget to show hospitality to strangers, for by so doing some people have shown hospitality to angels without knowing it."

I'm not saying this man was an angel, but wouldn't it be true to the nature of Jesus to stand in the rain as a homeless man to remind us that everyone has value?

He's always had a way of showing up in unexpected places.

THE PRESENT

My dad was a little like Doc Brown in "Back to the Future," minus the long hair and DeLorean. He loved clocks. He had several antique clocks that he had collected over the years and one "rescue" that he'd saved from the trash heap at his parents' estate.

But his pride and joy was a grandfather clock that stood in the den—and later in the dining room—until he passed away in 2013. It came as a kit in the mail from the Emperor Clock Company in June of 1975. A project that was supposed to take him and my mom a week or two consumed the better part of three months. Since my older siblings were no longer living at home, I was the one who ended up fetching tools, sweeping up wood chips, and otherwise shaking sawdust out of my hair for an entire summer that year.

One of the reasons this project took longer was because my dad was a perfectionist when it came to carpentry; hence the long, midsummer's night hours of sanding and weekends spent going to the hardware store. But the end result was a glowing reflection of his dedication to detail. The clock was a masterpiece, and its quarter-hour chiming punctuated many a memory in the years that followed.

My dad's obsession with timepieces was fitting, as he was always conscious of time and, specifically, time gone by. I'm beginning to think that this tendency toward the reflective is genetic. The older I get, the more I catch myself looking back, regaling my family with encore performances of "when I was growing up." They're continually amazed that the same woman who can't remember where she put her car keys can vividly recall events that happened decades ago.

On one occasion when I was mentally time traveling, I felt the Holy Spirit remind me that one day I'll be looking back on right now. I don't want to be so focused on yesterday's memories that I miss the ones being made today. And today is really all we have.

> *"This is the day the Lord has made; let us rejoice and be glad in it."*
>
> — PSALM 118:24

In His love and mercy, God gives us a chance to start over every twenty-four hours. Each morning when we wake up, it's a new opportunity to live the adventure of serving Him. It's a reminder to look forward and trust Him for what's ahead. That truly is a reason to rejoice and be glad.

The grandfather clock that my mom and dad worked so tirelessly to construct now proudly stands in my living room. While it's part of my heritage representing the past, it's also a reminder that today—right now—is a gift.

Maybe that's why it's called "the present."

GLACIER LIFE

With both of my daughters and my son-in-law living in Alaska, I attempt to visit as often as my schedule and budget will allow. My husband and I finally had a summer vacation planned where we'd see this beautiful state together. However, as I sat lamenting how far away July was (it was April at the time), I decided to make one more quick trip up there. My youngest daughter had a friend who was going to be visiting at the same time. With my two daughters, my son-in-law, a friend, two dogs, and me all under one roof, it was like the Alaskan version of Full House.

My youngest daughter loves the outdoors and everything that goes with it. Her dream life would be to live in an environment where she could have a vegetable garden, fetch water from a spring, and make her own soap. The fact that she has an overprotective mom really puts a damper on this picturesque existence. She currently has every feature imaginable on her cell phone so that I can keep up with her whereabouts. I've even considered installing a tracking device in one of her molars.

One way to ensure that she is safe is to go on adventures

with her. That's how I found myself on a tour of the Matanuska Glacier, which is located about 100 miles north-east of Anchorage. As we prepared to embark, the other tourists there were taking photos, laughing, and chatting with one another. I, on the other hand, was on the sidelines doing breathing exercises to calm my nerves. I could just picture spending my last moments on earth plummeting through millennium-old ice with nothing to mark my watery grave.

Before touring the Matanuska, I didn't know that much about glaciers except that an offshoot of one (i.e. an iceberg) sunk the Titanic. Now, I have a head full of glacial trivia. But only one thing really mattered while exploring this massive marine wonder: following the guide.

Our guide, Amy, had been leading tours on this glacier for over eighteen years and knew it like the back of her hand. She was adept at accessing the most breathtaking views while avoiding the dangers that lurked beneath. Since I was the "senior" member of our group, I chose to walk right behind Amy, stepping exactly where she stepped. This ensured that I would not only finish with all my limbs intact, but would enjoy the journey!

As we were finishing the tour (which had us traipsing through a glacial form of quick sand), I realized that glacier life is a lot like real life.

One similarity is the changing of the seasons. In late fall and winter, it's safe to tour the ice caves on a glacier since there's no chance of rivers suddenly gushing due to warming temperatures. However, the extreme cold makes the surface so hard that ice picks and Yaktrax shoes have little impact. Milder conditions in the spring and summer months make for a more pleasant expedition. There are small streams that wind their way along the crevices, showcasing clear water sparkling against blue ice. But the melting process necessitates that certain areas be off-limits, such as the caves. Each season has its beauty, as well as its challenges. The structure is constantly changing and shifting.

The most glaring similarity between glacier life and real life is that things aren't always as they seem. Danger is often camouflaged. One wrong move on something that looks solid (but isn't) could cause you to plummet hundreds of feet into certain hypothermia.

We spent a total of two hours on the Matanuska. The further we hiked, the more closely I followed Amy.

Real life is full of changes and can be unpredictable. Situations blindside us and, suddenly, we find ourselves down in a hole and we're not sure how we got there—or how to get out.

One of the most familiar scriptures in the Bible is Psalm 23. It begins with these verses: "The Lord is my shepherd, I lack nothing. He makes me lie down in green pastures, he leads me beside quiet waters, he refreshes my soul. He guides me along the right paths for his name's sake. Even though I walk through the darkest valley, I will fear no evil, for you are with me; your rod and your staff, they comfort me."

We all need the Shepherd to guide us on our journey. He has promised never to leave us nor forsake us. As we follow in His footsteps, we can be confident that we're going the right way, and that we have a solid foundation on which to stand. If we stray and fall, He's right there to pick us up.

Sunny weather and clear blue skies greeted me the day I flew back into North Carolina. Who knows what the conditions will be like weeks and months down the road?

My Shepherd does. And I'm letting Him take the lead.

LIONS AND TIGERS AND BEARS (AND SPIDERS)

While I love springtime, tolerate summer, and act like a kid when it snows in winter, autumn is my favorite season.

However, one part of this lovely time of year that I could do without is the noted increase in the spider population. The spiders in my neighborhood begin making a comeback as early as August. I remember one year, as I was taking a walk, I spotted two geometrically perfect webs along my route. In the dead center of each was the resident eight-legged homeowner/builder. While I managed to dodge both, my neighbor wasn't quite so lucky. Before I could warn him, he was doing karate chops in the air after plowing right into one.

After that experience, I shifted my path from the sidewalk to the nearby grass beside the street where, hopefully, the spiders wouldn't have anything they could attach their webs to. However, I've actually seen webs that appear to be suspended in midair. I'm not sure how these trapeze artists of the arachnid world manage this. The unsettling conclusion is that, no matter what precautions you take, nowhere is completely safe.

As I began pondering this dilemma, it dawned on me as to why small insects and other tiny pests bother us so much. It obviously isn't because they are bigger than us, or because we have no way to combat them. On the contrary, they are a mere fraction of our size, and all one needs is a good shoe, broom, or a can of Raid for a guaranteed victory.

I think what fundamentally bothers us is the fact that they *are* small and can creep in unnoticed. They can slip into your house without your ever knowing it. And while most aren't dangerous, a few are deadly. Bigger intruders would be much easier to detect. Here is a story I think will illustrate my point:

It's a Saturday morning. You wake up to the smell of coffee brewing. Your thoughts automatically go to your spouse who, evidently, arose early to start perking a fresh pot. You then hear the rattle of pots and pans. Now you're really impressed. Not only did your sweet husband make the coffee, but these sounds indicate that he is also preparing breakfast. But as you get up, you notice that your better half is still unshaven and snoring in bed next to you. You carefully descend the stairs and enter the kitchen where you're shocked to discover a tiger sitting at the counter and sipping on a cup of your French roast.

Intent on evicting this unwanted guest, you first employ diplomatic methods. You open the back door and issue directives such as "Shoo!" and "Go home!" To this, the tiger looks disinterested and proceeds to the refrigerator where he begins to take out the ingredients to make an omelet. You search the cabinet for your tranquilizer gun, which is conveniently located next to the bug spray. You aim at the tiger and in minutes he's purring peacefully. You check online for that Tiger Service everyone in the neighborhood has been raving about. A few minutes after dialing 1-800-Tiger-Out, the problem has been solved.

It's important to point out that later that same evening, you won't be lying in bed wondering if the tiger had cubs under your sheets. Or, if a tiger web will land on your face while you sleep. In short, there is no way the tiger can "slip back" into your house. And, in the rare event that it did, it would be easy to detect.

Similar to the odds of finding a tiger in your kitchen, the chances are slim to none that anyone reading this book will ever rob a bank or steal a car. But chances are good that we'll gossip in some form, harbor unforgiveness, or withhold love and mercy. These offenses won't land us in jail, but they certainly can cause us a few sleepless nights.

Jesus was radical in his approach to such matters. Unlike the Pharisees and teachers of the law, Jesus's focus wasn't as much on outward behavior, but on the attitudes of the heart. Like the spider that can construct a web in the dark and unseen places, hidden sins can grow unless we expose them to the light.

One way to prevent creepy things from forming in our hearts is to maintain regular fellowship with other believers. 1 John 1:7 instructs us that "if we walk in the light as he is in the light, we have fellowship with one another and the blood of Jesus Christ cleanses us from all sin."

Fellowship positions us for accountability and to receive the light and life of Christ that's living in others. We become inspired to do the things that keep us healthy and strong, such as reading scripture and spending time in prayer. And when sin is exposed, the precious blood of Christ provides cleansing and deliverance.

As I was rereading my story, I realized that the tiger must have made the coffee. Perhaps I should have let him go for the omelet. I wonder if he's free for lunch?

GIRL IN A DRAWER

Disclaimer: Do not try this at home. I wasn't a professional when I did this; I was just dumb. However, it does make for a humorous story.

As a child, I loved cartoons. I grew up in the pre-cable age, which meant we didn't have any of the networks that are so popular and accessible today. The average household television could only pick up three channels, and getting those to come in without fuzz and static was no easy feat. In addition to positioning the antenna on top of your television at just the right angle, there was another antenna on top of your house. A few brave dads would climb the roof and add tin foil to pick up a better signal. But regardless of how those moving pictures ended up on your screen, on Saturday mornings, they held the attention of children all across the U.S. of A.

For Saturday mornings were all about cartoons.

Back then, animated entertainment was safe and required no parental supervision. On any given Saturday, a mom could feed her baby boomer his or her breakfast and then know that for the next couple of hours, this child was in the trusted care of Bugs Bunny, the Road Runner, George Jetson, and the like.

Years later, when I had children of my own, the wholesome humor of the Flintstones and that smarter-than-average bear had been replaced by angry action figures with dark, supernatural powers. Pebbles and Bamm-Bamm singing "Let the Sunshine In" was replaced by expressionless children who regularly exuded negativity and sarcasm.

However, even the most innocent of children's shows can influence dangerous behavior. Such was the case when, after watching a cartoon where a mouse's little bed was the inside of a dresser drawer, I thought I'd give it a try. I'd like to say I was only two or three years old at the time and didn't know any better. But I was five. I knew better. I just wasn't thinking.

On a whim, I went into my parents' bedroom and removed the clothes from one of their dresser drawers. This drawer was at just the right height for me to crawl in. You don't have to be a physics major to figure out what happened next. The entire dresser began to topple over.

I remember yelling for help. My mom (who was a saint for putting up with all my shenanigans) ran into the room and rescued me from an untimely death-by-furniture. I wish I could recall the look on her face when she asked me *why* I was in the drawer. I only remember her getting me unwedged from the space between the drawer, the dresser, and their bed.

I've often thought about that day when I took leave of my senses, grateful for my mother's prompt response. The lesson I learned, besides the whole center-of-gravity principle, was that a place ideal for a cartoon mouse to bed down doesn't necessarily work for a five-year-old child.

While none of us would ever attempt such a circus act, how often do we do something similar? We see a celebrity on television or even a friend we admire. We want their lifestyle. We want their curly (or straight) hair. We wish we could live where they live or drive what they drive. Perhaps they get to travel and we don't. Whatever it is, we want what they have.

The Bible refers to this as coveting. In the lineup of the Ten Commandments, it's last, but it's certainly not least.

Exodus 20:17 instructs, "You shall not covet your neighbor's house. You shall not covet your neighbor's wife, or his male or female servant, his ox or donkey, or anything that belongs to your neighbor."

In case that verse isn't clear enough, let me sum it up for you. Don't covet.

Some of the dangers of coveting are obvious. We all know that coveting your neighbor's wife could lead to breaking commandment number seven, which is "You shall not commit adultery." However, there's also the "socially acceptable" variety. This form of coveting can be more toxic because it's harder to detect. It blends in seamlessly with the greed and sense of entitlement that's so prevalent in our culture today.

To overcome the temptation to covet, we need to rewind to the Garden of Eden where temptation, and the sin that resulted, made its debut. As we look at the dialogue between Eve and the serpent in Genesis chapter 3, we discover the enemy's tactics haven't changed all that much over the centuries. What he used on Eve, he still uses on us today. At the root of it all, he made Eve doubt God's goodness. Because if God isn't good, then it's every woman for herself. Eve believed the lie that God was holding out on her.

We all know He wasn't, but what if just the opposite was true? What if God was working on an expansion project? Scientific studies have proven that the universe is constantly expanding. What if those early chapters of Genesis were, truly, just the beginning?

Instead of having an infinite God provide for her infinitely, Eve chose her own way. But it wasn't what she was created for. She was created for more. When she crawled into that dresser drawer of her own making, what resulted was a fall. A big fall. The fall of mankind.

When our focus is on God's goodness and His abundant blessings in our lives, we won't be as apt to covet what others have. A grateful heart is already full and doesn't need to supplement. But when we do fall into temptation, we have a Savior who is always there to catch us and lead us back to safety.

My siblings, especially my sister, teased me for years about that fateful day when I was five. I still like dresser drawers that are extra roomy. But I'll sleep safely in my queen-size bed, thank you very much.

MOVING DAY

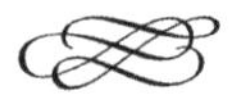

My husband and I have moved a total of eleven times during our thirty years of marriage. A few of these were to different houses within the same town, but a move all the same. We moved our oldest daughter seven times during her college career. My youngest daughter just completed move number three. So, as a family unit, we have collectively achieved twenty-one moves. And now that my oldest daughter has married into the military, we anticipate this number to increase exponentially.

Moving is exhausting, grueling work. However, I do remember hearing in a bedtime story as a child that there are companies who will do all this back-breaking labor for you. These fairy godmothers of the moving world will pack up your possessions and then deposit the loaded boxes into a large, climate-controlled van. We've never had this luxury, so moving day for our family continues to be defined by late-night trips to the drug store to pick up yet another tube of Icy Hot.

I caught a glimpse of a bumper sticker in traffic once that I thought summed it up quite eloquently. It was on a truck that looked like it had helped many a mattress and box spring find their new home. The bumper sticker simply read, "Yes, this is my truck. No, I will not help you move."

A move I'll never forget took place when my daughter was in college at Appalachian State, which is located in the mountain town of Boone, North Carolina. We were transferring her apartment furniture to a storage unit for the summer. With this project only involving a bedroom set, a desk, and some kitchen accessories, we thought we could handle it on our own. After all, how hard could it be?

However, upon our return, we looked like we had just stepped off the set of *Gladiator*. While we were calculating our ability to accomplish this feat without additional manpower, we neglected to factor in her apartment being eye level with low-flying aircraft. Had I planned better, I would have brought along oxygen for the endless flights of stairs we had to navigate in order to transport her belongings.

But for me, the worst part of moving isn't just the lifting and carrying of items that require a follow-up appointment with a chiropractor. It's the scary sights you discover while cleaning afterward. Without a coroner, it would be impossible to determine the time of death of the granola bar that is found where your child's dresser once stood. Or, how about the dust bunnies so large that you suspect metabolic steroids were involved?

We all know we wouldn't have to be afraid of what's lurking behind the washing machine if we would slide it out periodically and do a little investigating. Sometimes we hit a situation in life where everything is moved around and the accumulated dust and dirt overwhelm us. If we would take the time to pray and ask God to show us where maintenance is needed on a daily basis, these issues could be dealt with on a much smaller scale.

"Your word is a lamp to my feet and a light to my path." And Psalm 19:8 teaches us, "The precepts of the Lord are right, giving joy to the heart. The commands of the Lord are radiant, giving light to the eyes."

— PSALM 119:105

God's word brings illumination to our paths and exposes the cobwebbed corners of our hearts. His truth will uncover anything hidden. And with it, He brings cleansing, forgiveness, and joy as we apply it to our lives.

Regarding the dust bunnies, up in the mountains they resemble dust bears. Parents of students at Appalachian State, proceed with caution!

OUTWARD APPEARANCES

From the time they were toddlers until my oldest daughter left for college, my two children had their picture taken each year for the family Christmas card. In the early days, I used a professional photographer. But as the years (and technology) progressed, I took the picture myself and had the cards printed at a local department store.

I'm sure that when our friends and loved ones received our greeting in the mail with my two cherubs smiling in their holiday attire, they were filled with the Christmas spirit. Perhaps they were taken back to when they, themselves, were children and were joyfully anticipating the magic of the season. In movie reel fashion, they'd envision me putting the finishing touches on my little ones' dresses as we listened to Christmas carols. Occasionally we would pause to hang yet another shining ornament on the tree. The fragrance of apple cider simmering on the stove filled the room, as a gentle snow fell outside. The scene would be made complete by the family dog napping by the fireplace.

What really happened?

That fateful day started off with a weather report

predicting unseasonably warm temperatures. Before they were fully awake, my children were already whining about having to get their picture taken. In a moment of weakness and desperation, I resorted to bribing them with a trip to Chuck E. Cheese's if they promised to sit still for the camera.

Breakfast was punctuated by my youngest daughter crying as she threw her food at the dog from her high chair. The rest of it she put in her hair. I frantically whisked her into the bathtub while my oldest daughter began to dress herself, forgetting to wash her hands after breakfast. I sprinted into her room with my younger daughter wrapped up in a towel and tucked under my arm like a football. In the nick of time, I rescued the white, starched blouse from further defilement by grape jelly fingers.

The next phase of the morning constituted department-of-social-services-worthy screaming as I tried to brush and, God forbid, curl their hair. We were finally on our way out the door when we heard the unmistakable sound of the dog throwing up on the living room carpet.

We all want our lives to resemble that Christmas card picture we send out each year. We regularly strive to make it look like we have it all together. We sanitize the bathrooms before the in-laws visit and brush our teeth for twenty minutes prior to each dentist appointment. And while none of us would want to greet our hygienist with chicken remnants wedged between our molars, the reality is that we don't dust every day and sometimes go to bed without flossing.

The good news is that when it comes to inviting Jesus in, we don't have to clean up first or wait until everything is neat and tidy. The Bible teaches us that Jesus stands at the door of our hearts and knocks. He's fully aware of the piles of dirty laundry and unswept floors that wait on the other side. In fact, he wouldn't knock if he didn't know we needed him to come in and remodel. He understands that we are incapable of doing it on our own.

In Matthew 11:28-30 Jesus says, "Come unto me all you that are weary and burdened and I will give you rest. Take my yoke upon you and learn from me, for I am gentle and humble in heart, and you shall find rest for your souls. For my yoke is easy and my burden is light."

His offer is for us to hang up our brooms and dustpans in exchange for His gift of forgiveness and salvation. Then we are promised that our sins will become as white as that Christmas snow that we all dream about.

TSUNAMI

As adults, we often wonder where some of our fears and hang-ups originated. For instance, I still don't know why I was afraid of coyotes as a child. I'd only seen them in the movies. Our street was three blocks from town, so there was a low probability of a coyote just randomly showing up at my house. Yet, I was convinced that one lived under my bed. It still doesn't make sense. However, there was another fear that tormented me, and I know exactly where it came from. For this one, I have to point a finger at Dear Old Dad.

For many years, I was terrified of thunderstorms. I can trace it back to my dad telling (and retelling) the tale of an older relative who was struck by lightning. Twice. While this account was true, other warnings that my parents issued to my siblings and me were, let's just say, less than reliable.

Here are just a few:

1. If you eat paper (never a temptation for me), you'll get worms.

2. If you walk barefoot, you'll get worms. (What was it with worms?)
3. If you cross your eyes, they'll get stuck that way.
4. Popping your knuckles will cause you to have arthritis.

Having raised two kids, I can now understand how a concerned and frustrated parent can resort to bribery, exaggeration, and other desperate measures to maintain the health and well-being of their children. For example, having swallowed a piece of hard candy as a little girl, I forbade my own children from ever having any. In fact, my grown daughters still refer to cough drops as "choke candy."

We can't protect our children from all of life's dangers and hardships. But we can teach them how to not only survive the storms, but also benefit from them.

One thing I've learned about storms is that when you're in the middle of one, you forge ahead with adrenaline much like you would if you were in a real-life threat to your survival. However, something we aren't always prepared for is what can happen *afterward.* Similar to a tsunami that follows an earthquake, the full effect doesn't always set in until the incident has passed.

We all know that a tsunami is a gigantic surge of water that occurs after a geological event, such as an earthquake. If the earthquake takes place out in the middle of the ocean, it may or may not affect human life. However, the tsunami that follows can be devastating.

The aftermath of dealing with a difficult situation can sometimes be worse than the situation itself. Emotions that have been put on ice begin to thaw. Fatigue or other health issues that have been ignored now vie for our attention. Isaiah 43:1-2 brings us comfort in those times.

> *"But now, thus says the LORD, your Creator, O Jacob, And He who formed you, O Israel, do not fear, for I have redeemed you; I have called you by name; you are mine! When you pass through the waters, I will be with you; And through the rivers, they will not overflow you."*

Even when we may feel as though we are being battered by a tidal wave, God is still in control. Not only is He with us during these challenging seasons, but He has promised that the waters will not overtake us.

With this understanding, instead of fearing the storms (as I did as a child), we can stand in awe of God's glory displayed in them. The one who created such a demonstration of His power is both Defender and Redeemer. He is on our side, working all things together for our good. Whether the sky is clear or there are clouds in the distance, we can rest assured that we are always safe and secure in the palm of His hand.

DON'T SWEAT THE BIG FISH

I've always been a worrier. It started when I was a child. I worried about all sorts of things, not the least of which was a spider or a bug crawling into my bed and eating me while I was asleep. I also worried about my older siblings telling on me for something that I did, or didn't, do. In an ongoing effort to console me, my dad would shake his head and say, "Don't worry until you have something to worry about." (Such as being struck by lightning. See the previous chapter.)

A friend of mine, who is also a worrier, has a habit of getting expressions such as this one mixed up with others like it. For example, one on occasion she meant to say, "I felt like a fifth wheel." Instead, she blurted out, "I felt like I was walking on three legs."

In keeping with her endearing propensity for butchering metaphors, I considered two that apply to worrying. The first is "Don't sweat the small stuff." The other is "You've got bigger fish to fry." Combine the two, and you've arrived at the title of this devotional.

It's interesting how the sages of the world, including our parents, instruct us to not fret over the little things in life. As a six-year-old, there really wasn't a reason for me to stress over a roach making a nocturnal meal of me. How about me getting my ponytail pulled by that mean kid on the playground? Chances are good this wouldn't have resulted in a national catastrophe, or even something I'd remember by the time I entered the fourth grade.

We're told not to worry about the small things in life. But does that permit us to do so about the big things? Are we saying that there is a time to worry? How big does a problem have to be before we embrace the fear and stress that cause those pesky gray hairs and stomach ulcers? When do we *sweat the big fish?*

Now, I realize the image of yourself stressing over a large, aquatic creature to the point where you're literally sweating is a bit horrifying. In fact, it's downright silly. But scripture teaches us that worrying is just that. Silly. However, when someone we love gets cancer, worrying seems like the reasonable thing to do. Or when our teenager starts dating "that guy," isn't it our responsibility to pace the floors? When is it our duty to sweat the big fish?

In Luke 12:25-26, Jesus says, "Who of you by worrying can add a single hour to your life? Since you cannot do this very little thing, why do you worry about the rest?"

Scripture is clear that when it comes to worrying, it's one-size-fits-all. Regardless of the magnitude of the situation, our focus is to be placed on the magnitude of our God. He cares about the minnows as well as the whales that we wrestle. To Him, it's all doable. All things are possible.

The next time you're tempted to worry, remember that in 1 Peter 5:7, we're instructed to "cast all your anxiety on him because he cares for you." Like fish we've caught that we don't want to keep, may we not hold onto our problems, regardless of their size. May we offer them to our Savior who never grows tired or weary and can handle the little—and the big—fish without ever breaking a sweat!

UNDER QUALIFIED

I have a bad habit of starting projects for which I am under qualified. Over the years, this tendency has necessitated numerous visits to Urgent Care or the Emergency Room where I have had fingers sewn up and x-rays taken of most of my appendages. But it would only take one tantalizing window treatment to make me forget the pain of dropping a dresser on my foot and be inspired to hop back in the project-saddle once again.

My proudest achievement was when I refinished our back staircase. This began with the removal of several thousand staples that evidently are required to hold eight feet of carpet in place. By the time I was done, I looked like I had been attacked by a large cat. The next step was the sanding and staining, which I also did myself. While the end result looked good enough, the drawback was how long it took me. A carpenter could have done the job in two days. It took me every bit of three weeks.

When I had recovered from that project, I decided to tackle the front staircase. This staircase is larger and, well, is in the front of the house. So, it definitely had to look like a professional had done the job. I had just begun the process when my oldest daughter came to my work site. She took note of the pile of sharp tools on the floor beside me and, more importantly, the look in my eyes that was unrealistically optimistic. Her response was, "I really don't have time to take you to the emergency room today."

I knew she meant business. Therefore, I only went as far as removing the existing carpet. Afterward, I called my neighbor, who is a general contractor. He did the carpentry work and then had one of his painters complete the sanding and staining. It was amazing how great it looked, and we didn't even have to be concerned if our medical deductible had been met.

How often do we attempt to do God's job? I think it goes without saying how under qualified we are, and yet how often do we still try? This is evidenced by our worrying, fretting, and having our emotions feel as though they've been hit by a round of carpet staples. As hard as it can be to release certain situations to our Heavenly Father, it's even harder to deal with the fallout from trying to fix them on our own. We usually make a mess of it before we allow Him to come and do things His way and in His timing.

In 1 Peter 5:7, we're instructed to "Give all your worries and cares to God, for He cares about you."

When situations are bigger than we are, we have a God who can handle it. We just need to let Him do it.

My family has been aware of my biting-off-more-than-I-can-chew propensity for years. In fact, when my father passed away, my siblings lovingly suggested that I take his old wheelchair home with me. At the rate I was going, they figured I had three more projects before I would sustain an injury that would impair my mobility. But by that time, I had learned my limitations.

Besides, there was no way I could maneuver a wheelchair on that back set of stairs. And as hard as I had worked, I was determined to walk up and down them for as long as possible.

BLUE JAY BLUES

When I think of my favorite birds, I think of the melodious robin that serenades us on a warm spring morning. I consider the handsome cardinal, his feathery, red coat in stark contrast to a snowy, winter background. I also enjoy hearing the hoot of an owl on a crisp autumn evening when he calls to another in a nearby tree. Even though blue is my favorite color, I rarely put the blue jay in my lineup. Why? Because blue jays aren't exactly known for their random acts of kindness.

These bullies of the bird species remind me of the lead characters in the movie *Mean Girls*. They're pretty, you're supposed to like them, but they appear to take every opportunity to intimidate those they consider to be beneath them. And when it comes to these otherwise majestic flying creatures, everyone is *literally* beneath them.

My first encounter with a blue jay was when I was a teen. I had a cat that was constantly harassed by one. I tried to scare it away on numerous occasions by waving my arms and yelling. But nothing seemed to deter the relentless onslaught of dive-bomb-pecking.

If the internet had been invented back then, I would have discovered that I wasn't alone in my feud de fowl. Recently, I did a little online research. In doing so, I discovered that these birds not only attack other birds and small animals, but humans as well. I also learned that they have a complex social structure and tight family bonds. I don't know about you, but that screeches *bird mafioso* to me.

To make matters worse, the Migratory Bird Treaty Act of 1918 prohibits anyone from disturbing their habitat. Apparently, whoever passed that law hadn't dealt with a blue jay firsthand. Or, perhaps this public official was "strong-winged" into it. I picture an older, sage-looking, bespectacled gentleman tied to a chair and mercilessly pelted with seed until he signed on the dotted line.

Blue jays can be compared to the small, pesky sins or habits in our lives. If a blue jay momentarily perches on your favorite tree, it's not a big deal. But if it builds a nest and begins to torment your cat, you've got a problem.

The key is to learn how to deal with these trespassers before they establish a permanent residence in your backyard. The same is true with sin. The occasional "I'm only telling you this so you can pray about it" can turn into a tendency to gossip. The quick look at an inappropriate website can develop into a pornography addiction. If sin isn't dealt with in its infancy, but is fed and allowed to grow, it can become a serious issue that results in widespread heartache and destruction.

The book of James addresses this in chapter 1, verses 13-15: "When tempted, no one should say, 'God is tempting me.' For God cannot be tempted by evil, nor does he tempt anyone; but each person is tempted when they are dragged away by their own evil desire and enticed. Then, after desire has conceived, it gives birth to sin; and sin, when it is full-grown, gives birth to death."

An effective battle plan begins with avoiding situations that might cause us to fall to begin with. It's also essential that we renew our minds daily through scripture reading and memorization. This cleanses us from our own fallen thinking and aligns us with the life-giving truth of God's word. And, finally, we all need someone to whom we can hold ourselves accountable. Having a pastor or friend we can talk to helps us avoid land mines we might not otherwise be aware of.

Regarding the birds that sport my favorite color, I still don't know the best way to evict them. I've read articles suggesting the use of wind chimes or a rubber snake. If I'm ever forced to deal with one again, I've considered offering this songbird a song of my own. After hearing my not-so-melodious voice lamenting my state of duress, it would definitely be the blue jay singing the blues.

LINT ROLLER

Both of my parents grew up during the Great Depression. As a result, they taught my siblings and me how to make do with what we had, particularly when it came to gadgets and non-necessities. For instance, a broom handle doubled as a paint roller extension. Before they could afford to buy luggage, my parents packed for trips using the old-fashioned, sturdy, paper sacks from the grocery store. We didn't own a lint roller, so removing lint or pet hair from our clothes was accomplished by applying a piece of masking tape.

My children grew up in a different world. Not only were their big needs met, but small ones were indulged as well. I remember the night of my oldest daughter's senior prom. She was in the middle of putting on her make-up when she couldn't find a sharpener for her eyeliner. This little gadget is like other things that when you don't need one, you see them everywhere. Every drawer you open is going to have a pencil sharpener. You'll find one in the dryer, or discover one in the refrigerator wedged between the butter and the salad dressing. But when it's prom night and your daughter's makeup needs to be on point, there isn't one to be found in the entire house.

Ignoring the voice in my head telling me how ridiculous it was, I went to the store anyway and returned with four. (We may not be able to find a safety pin, but by gosh, we weren't going to be short an eyeliner sharpener ever again!) My folks wouldn't have responded like that. To the contrary, I can remember standing in my parents' kitchen sharpening a number two pencil with a steak knife. (It may not have been the *safest* method, but again, we made do.)

Another difference is how we provide for our pets. When I was a child, dogs and cats lived outside, and their diets consisted mostly of table scraps. We didn't know any different, and neither did they. Now we feed our pets kibble formulated for their specific breed. We buy them expensive toys and provide them with quality healthcare. And let's not forget the clothes. I've seen poodles at the vet with better wardrobes than mine!

Whenever I travel to visit to my daughter, son-in-law, and their four-legged offspring, I always return with what amounts to a small area rug of dog hair on my clothes. Skipping the lint roller step, I usually just toss the canine coiffure-covered garments into the dirty clothes hamper. What the wash cycle doesn't take care of, the dryer lint trap usually does. Occasionally I'll find a stubborn hair or two that's resisted. While sporting a bulldog's coat on my coat isn't exactly fashion-forward, I really don't mind. Since they live over three thousand miles away in Alaska, it's like having a small part of them with me.

Not long ago, we had a heartbreaking situation with my daughter's French Bulldog, Gatsby. My husband and I had just spent nine days vacationing with the family in Alaska. It was a fun time for everyone, including the dogs. While the humans enjoyed hiking and touring, Gatsby and his "sister," an English Bulldog named Daisy, enjoyed endless games of fetch. The highlight of the trip —for both species— was a trip to Mirror Lake. Not only was the scenery breathtaking, but also the sight of Gatsby and Daisy running in and out of the shallow water is one I'll always treasure. Gatsby, in particular, was having the time of his life. Little did he know, that day his life was about to change. It was the last time he would ever run on his own.

Shortly after we touched down in North Carolina, I received word from my daughter that a back problem Gatsby had suffered from some months earlier had returned. It was a serious situation that required emergency surgery. There was still a chance that he wouldn't recover the voluntary use of his back legs. He was only three years old at the time and full of life and energy.

As the days and weeks passed following Gatsby's surgery, his incision began to heal. But my heart didn't. I continued to long for that day at Mirror Lake when he had use of all four legs. I would look at the remaining dog hair that was still stuck to the sweater I wore that afternoon. I knew I needed to get the lint roller and clean it off, but I couldn't. It was all I had left from that seemingly perfect moment in time.

Then I began to realize that the pain went much deeper than grieving the physical limitations of a beloved pet. There had been other heartaches in recent years, such as losing my mom to a ten-year battle with Alzheimer's, and watching my dad suffer in his last moments from congestive heart failure. I wanted to relive seeing the joy in my mom's face when the grandkids would arrive for a visit. Or, to once again hear my dad sing off-key in church. I longed for the simpler days when my kids were growing up. The problems back then were bite-sized; the most we had to worry about were runny noses, homework, and whose turn it was to drive for carpool.

When life deals an unexpected blow, we want to be able to turn back the clock to when things made sense. We want answers to help us regain our footing. Sometimes those answers come, and sometimes they don't. It's in these times that we need to pull out the piece of our spiritual armor we often leave in the closet —the helmet of hope.

> *"But since we belong to the day, let us be sober, putting on faith and love as a breastplate, and the hope of salvation as a helmet."*
>
> — 1 THESSALONIANS 5:8

Hope, like a helmet, is something that protects our minds. When life gets tough, it's hard to see past the pain of the present. Hope gives us something to look forward to. Different from wishful thinking, Biblical hope is based on the truth of God's word and the unchanging nature of His character. Hope challenges us to take our eyes off the temporal and focus on the eternal. We can have peace even if we don't have an explanation. The problems might not go away, but we become reliant on a God who is bigger than our problems.

I eventually pulled out the lint roller and cleaned off that sweater. I'm still holding onto the memories from that day, but I've let go of the pain. It's a new day, and it's time to make new memories. In fact, I've already started planning my next trip to Alaska where, once again, I'll spend time with Gatsby and Daisy. Of course, whatever I wear will get dog hair all over it.

And if I can't find my lint roller, a piece of masking tape will work just fine.

THE POO CHAIR

A common icebreaker at parties is, "What was your most embarrassing moment?" But let's face it, people rarely disclose their most embarrassing moment. The majority of us only share what we feel comfortable sharing. The point is to not further embarrass ourselves. It was bad enough the first time around, right?

I can remember the first time I was truly embarrassed. It was a typical Monday morning in Miss Justice's first grade classroom. After snack time, the next hour was devoted to reading groups. The class was divided up based on reading skills. Several other students and I had been placed in the top group.

Disclaimer: Language Arts was always my best subject. Math, on the other hand, was something that I would fail at —literally—for the rest of my life. People tend to fall into one of two categories: those who are predominantly left-brained and those who are predominantly right-brained. The right side of my brain works just fine. However, I picture the left side of my brain as not merely low-functioning, but more like the closed section of a restaurant that is roped off and the power disconnected.

All seven or eight of us in my group were asked to sit down in little wooden chairs that were arranged in a circle. After a couple of minutes into her lesson, Miss Justice (her real name) was interrupted by her top reading students making noises like, "Ewww!" and asking, "What's that smell?"

Now, let me be clear that, while we may have only been six years old, we knew what the smell was. This wasn't rocket science.

As the youngest of three children, I was already a veteran at being blamed for things I hadn't done. Like an approaching rain shower, I could smell an "I'm gonna tell Mama that you said a bad word if you tell her I just drank the last Pepsi," from a mile away. In all fairness, my older siblings redeemed themselves later in life. However, they took advantage of my being the smallest, and not street-wise regarding family politics, and basically blackmailed me for the first decade of my life. But this morning, I was innocent, and I was going to prove it.

After examining the bottoms of our shoes, we each began to stand up and look in our chairs. That's when the unthinkable happened. *My* chair had poo in it. I cannot adequately describe how mortified I felt. I knew I wasn't responsible for this untimely bowel release, but I still felt defiled. Miss Justice defended my honor by finding the true culprit and taking us both to the bathroom where we were provided with soap and water and a change of clothes.

By this time, I'm sure you're thinking, this is sort of cute, and yet gross. What's the point?

Sometimes in life, we get the chair with the poo in it. Things happen that are beyond our control and aren't our fault. People make mistakes that affect us in negative ways. It can be something as simple as a careless word or as devastating as sexual abuse. But we walk around in soiled clothes, bearing the stench of someone else's behavior.

Miss Justice had the solution. She helped to clean me up and gave me fresh clothes to wear. Now, let me pause for a minute and ask a question. What if I had decided not to let my teacher help me? What if I decided to go back to my desk in that condition? Sounds ridiculous, right?

Yet, in life, we have a choice of what to do about the poo chair we may have sat in. We can hold on to the pain and unforgiveness, or we can avail ourselves to the One who knows how to clean us up and give us a fresh start. Jesus came to heal the brokenhearted. He came not only to forgive sin but also to provide healing from the *effects* of sin. He can bring cleansing where we have been made to feel dirty. And when we give him our heart, all things become new. It's like we get a fresh change of clothes on the inside.

The story of my sitting in the poo chair is one that my family chuckled about for years. It was often said, "This could have only happened to you!" Now, years later, I'm glad that it did. While it did teach me that "sit happens" (couldn't resist that one), it taught me so much more.

NAME CHANGE

Years ago, there was an old television show that began with the disclaimer, "The story you are about to see is true. The names have been changed to protect the innocent."

The producers of this series could have included the names of these victims for my viewing, and they would have been perfectly safe. I hold the equivalent of an Olympic gold medal for both forgetting names and slaughtering their pronunciations. You can tell me your name, and five minutes later I'll sheepishly ask you to repeat it. Or, if I'm feeling adventurous, I'll cross my fingers and call you what I think you just said. In either case, I routinely get it wrong. And that's if we're family. For strangers, it can take months or even years before your name and face permanently connect in my brain.

My knack for forgetting names runs in my family. Not only did my dad call the guy I was dating at one time "Tom" (his name was Bob), but he would call me by my aunt's name, my sister's name, and my mother's name before finally arriving at my name. At times, it was reminiscent of a reading of an Old Testament genealogy account.

In scripture, names and their meanings are important, which is why we have those seemingly endless lists of who begat whom. Personally, I have always felt bad for the Old Testament kids whose names represented a less-than-favorable state of the union. Ichabod (pronounced Ick-a-bod) stands out most to me in that category. It means "the glory has departed." I'm sure middle school was tough enough back in ancient Israel without being the young man saddled with the name "Ichabod."

Name *changes* were also significant. A name change would take place when someone's destiny was about to be transformed. God changed Abram's and Sarai's names to include the letter 'H' which, in Hebrew, represents God's Spirit. (We know them better as Abraham and Sarah.) This signified that, going forward, their destinies wouldn't be limited to what they could do in their own human abilities. God had just been inserted into the equation and, with Him, all things are possible.

Abraham was referred to as "the friend of God." If you have ever identified yourself as a loser, a misfit, a failure, or any of the above, I have good news for you. God wants to give you a new name. Jesus loved you so much that He took your sins upon himself. He rose from the dead so you could have newness of life. When you accept this gift, your destiny will change. And so will your name. God wants to call you "friend."

I am continuing to work on my name recollection skills. If we are ever introduced, I will probably have to ask you to repeat your name. If I keep getting it wrong, feel free to just say your name is "Friend." I'll know exactly who you are.

LOOKING UP

What if I told you that one Halloween when I was a child, we had the coolest jack-o-lantern on our block? You would probably picture an exquisitely carved gourd proudly displayed on our front porch. Or, if I told you that we had a cat that gave birth to a litter of kittens, you would assume this act of nature occurred in a quiet, secluded place, like the basement. Both are logical assumptions. However, since we are talking about *my* family, both are incorrect.

I'll never forget the Halloween that my dad, an electrician by trade, wired a light bulb up to the roof and set our jack-o-lantern on top of the chimney. Our house was on a hill, so trick-or-treaters could enjoy this orange, toothy glow from a good distance away. At one point during the evening, my dad had to adjust the whole set-up. Stories and speculations were in no short supply in the days and weeks that followed regarding a tall, spooky figure moving around on the roof of our house that night.

But the rooftop chronicles don't end there. Another had to do with a cat named Nancy. I need to pause here and insert that years ago, pet owners didn't spay and neuter their cats and dogs like they do today. And, evidently, the feline population in our neighborhood was quite fertile.

Nancy, who was an outside cat, had become pregnant by a stealthy Casanova down the street. The time for her to deliver had come and gone with no sign of the kittens. The mystery was solved one day when we spotted Nancy bringing her new litter, one kitten at a time, down a tree in our yard whose branches extended over the roofline. We soon learned that Nancy had given birth in the gutter on the roof. Looking back, that was one smart cat. There were several dogs in our neighborhood that were not cat-friendly. Evidently, Nancy knew that dogs couldn't climb trees. Her prudent choice kept her babies out of harm's way.

Both of these occurrences extended beyond the realm of the usual and the predictable, which is most likely why my family still remembers them. In both instances, to enjoy the wonder of it all, we had to look up.

But what if we hadn't?

What if, after not seeing a jack-o-lantern on our front porch that night, I had become disappointed or even upset when, in reality, my father had a surprise for me that would exceed my expectations? And what if our cat's instincts hadn't prompted her to choose such a safe (albeit unconventional) birthing place? Her kittens could have been harmed or even killed.

Sometimes the answers we're seeking to resolve life's challenges aren't visible at eye level. We have to look up. The usual formulas and methods that we've relied on in the past simply aren't working this time. In these faith-stretching seasons, our Heavenly Father is reminding us that He is the ultimate source of wisdom and guidance. He wants us to look beyond the problem and ourselves and allow Him to show us His plan.

James 1:5 teaches us that "If any of you lacks wisdom, he should ask of God who gives generously to all without finding fault, and it will be given to you."

Who better to provide us with a creative solution than the Creator Himself? And His plans for us will *always* exceed our expectations.

DEEP FREEZE

In the movie *Home Alone,* young Kevin McAllister was afraid to go into the basement because of the menacing furnace lurking in the shadows. That's how I felt about my parents' basement. It was unfinished and used for miscellaneous storage. Over the years, it also became home to a deep freezer located at the opposite corner of the room from the door. It couldn't have been more than a few yards away, but it felt farther. Traveling from the door to the deep freezer could have been a precursor to another television favorite, *Survivor.*

First of all, there were no stairs leading down to the basement from the inside; you had to go outside and around the house. My parents kept the door locked, and it would consistently stick when you tried to unlock it. Several key jiggles were usually required before it finally surrendered. Just inside the door and to the right was a Texas Chainsaw Massacre assortment of lawn and garden tools ranging from shovels and rakes to hatchets and pickaxes, all covered in spider webs. Straight ahead was a dusty maple chest of drawers, riddled with borer worm holes, that a friend of the family handcrafted back in the '70s.

My journey through the gauntlet continued as I had to navigate around old wheelbarrows, a lawn mower, and several open boxes of Christmas decorations. One box contained a large, battery-operated Santa doll whose eyes seemed to follow me as I made my way over to the freezer. I would grab whatever barbeque or Brunswick stew that I had been sent to fetch and would quickly exit, wildly brushing off my clothes whether they needed it or not.

Growing up, I never quite understood the purpose of a deep freezer. In my predominately right-brained thinking, frozen was frozen. Why not just keep everything upstairs where it is convenient (and safe) to access? Then I learned that a deep freezer keeps food frozen at a much colder temperature, and food stored at that temperature can be stored longer, and it seals in the nutrients better than some other methods of food preservation.

Whenever it gets really cold in the winter, it reminds me of the term deep freeze. My parents were always glad when we would get at least one "cold snap," as they called it, when the temperature would drop low enough to kill off harmful pests, such as mosquitoes. I wasn't sure how that of all worked (or if it worked at all), but I was always in favor of anything that would get rid of bugs. When a deep freeze happens outside, it's a reminder about life. We may already think it's cold enough, and then it gets even colder. We're certain that we have more on our plates than we can handle, and then something else lands there.

I will always remember my 40th birthday, if for no other reason than the fact that it occurred on Friday the 13th. Since I'm not superstitious, I actually found this to be an example of God's sense of humor. When I got up that morning to run errands, I had a flat tire. (I can't make this stuff up!) I managed to drive a short distance up the street to have it changed. When I arrived, I jokingly remarked to the mechanic, "Can this day get any worse?" He quickly reminded me, "It can always get worse."

Sometimes when we're in the middle of a crisis, we think the situation can't get any worse, and then it does. You already have a teen who's causing you worry and heartache, and then he or she gets into trouble again. You're struggling with your own health, and then your spouse gets sick. How do we deal with going from the freezer to the deep freeze? When we're already feeling overwhelmed, how can we cope with even more stress?

In the Old Testament, we read about a man named Job who loved God and was the most upright man of his time. One day, a series of tragedies caused him to lose his land, livestock, children, and, eventually, his health. With each report of bad news, the situation worsened. He had friends who tried both to console him and to figure out why these things had happened. Job never cursed God throughout his ordeal. He did, however, have questions, as we all would have.

I find it interesting that when God appeared to Job in chapter 38, He didn't answer any of Job's questions. Rather, He asked questions of Job, requiring him to remember who He was and all that He had done as his Creator and Sustainer. Job became so immersed in the presence of God that answers were no longer necessary. He was reminded that He served a mighty and powerful God who ultimately was in control, whether Job understood everything or not. What Satan intended as a means to destroy Job, God used to bring him to a deeper level of intimacy with Himself.

In the end, God restored all that Job had lost—with interest! The latter part of Job's life was better than the first. He lived to a ripe old age with more wealth and with a larger family than he had before. The most important thing he gained, however, was a new level of rest in the sovereignty of God. He learned that there is no substitute for drawing near to God, not just for answers, but because He's worthy of our trust. And when our eyes are focused on the One who created the universe, those mountains in our path don't seem quite so big.

As we brace ourselves for winter's cold temperatures, we can be thankful for roofs over our heads and warm clothes to wear. If you don't have a deep freezer for those extra items you might want to store, perhaps your back porch will suffice.

And it's not as creepy as the basement.

THE PIG NEXT DOOR

My family has always been supportive of the armed forces. My father was a World War II Navy veteran. He was a true patriot who was honored to have served his country. My brother followed as a proud member of the National Guard. When my oldest daughter married a West Point graduate, we became even more aware of the sacrifices military families make. One is the frequent packing up and relocating for the next assignment. Of course, this necessitates that new living arrangements be made each time.

When my daughter's husband received orders for training in Oklahoma, they got the last house that was available. They were grateful for a roof over their heads, but it wasn't what they would have picked out. So, as soon as they found out their next move would be to Alaska, they began house hunting.

Their early shopping paid off. They found a lovely home with lots of room, new appliances, and a beautiful mountain view from the backyard. However, there was one detail left out of the rental agreement, something that they hadn't planned on—or bargained for. And that was the pig that lived next door.

Let me be clear that, when I say pig, I mean *pig*; a large, pot-bellied, oinking pig. The first time they suspected their neighbors owned an omnivore was when they heard the clicking of cloven hooves on the deck next door. These neighbors also had two dogs. Evidently one of them resented the fact that a walking slab of bacon slept on the floor next to him. On more than one occasion, when the pig would try to enter through the back sliding-glass door (which the owners left partially open), the dog would take the opportunity to establish who was the alpha species. The result was a most unpleasant (and loud) cacophony of barking and squeals.

At first, I sided with the pig. After all, it wasn't his fault the whole blended family thing wasn't working in his favor. Then I reconsidered. I'd seen my daughter's two dogs at the fence gazing at this breakfast side dish sunning himself in the backyard. Perhaps it was humiliating for his canine sibling to cohabitate with something deemed as "the other white meat." Perhaps the neighborhood dogs gave him a hard time for it. Either way, it often made for a thought-provoking—and entertaining—conversation topic.

When I arrived back home from a visit there, I continued to ponder this whole pig-next-door thing. It reminded me of a parable Jesus told in Matthew chapter 7:3-5. "Why do you look at the speck of sawdust in your brother's eye and pay no attention to the plank in your own eye? How can you say to your brother, 'Let me take the speck out of your eye,' when all the time there is a plank in your own eye? You hypocrite, first take the plank out of your own eye, and then you will see clearly to remove the speck from your brother's eye."

Before we criticize our neighbor for having a pet pig, perhaps we need to recognize the "pigs" we've fed and allowed to reside in *our* homes. For example, perhaps our short temper and harsh words don't sunbathe in front of the whole neighborhood. Instead, we unleash them privately behind closed doors. It's so easy for us to judge what we think is an obvious weakness in others, when, in reality, we carry the weightier sin.

Someone once said Jesus used the eye as a reference point because it's so sensitive. Even a tiny lash that's fallen in can cause a lot of pain. It's important that we first experience the crucifixion of sin in our own lives, so we can understand how much it hurts. Then, when we seek to help our neighbor remove the sin in his life, we'll be better equipped. Our touch will be a little gentler, our methods more merciful.

I never caught the name of the pig next door. For his sake, I hope he *had* a name and wasn't just food insurance for the long, Alaskan winter that lay ahead. Maybe I'll think twice before I eat that yummy slice of ham this holiday season.

Then again, maybe not.

FIRST THANKSGIVING

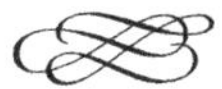

Even though I'm certain I tripped over a plastic candy cane while buying sunscreen back in August, the stores are now officially teeming with Christmas decorations. With the overlap in marketing, it is odd to see Santa, angels, and snowflakes just aisles away from scarecrows and the Grim Reaper. And unless you're in a grocery store, one holiday that doesn't seem to get equal representation is that holiday that, as my sister once pointed out, tends to be the speed bump between the two: Thanksgiving.

Thanksgiving has always been one of my favorite holidays. I have fond memories of being in elementary school and learning about—and dressing up like—the Pilgrims and the Native Americans. It was like picking a team as to which costume you would wear. If I remember correctly, the girls favored the black and white construction paper Pilgrim attire, while the boys preferred the colorful feathers and fringed paper vests consistent with Native American wear.

Another favorite childhood memory of mine was waking up to the smell of a slow-cooked turkey. My mom always put ours in the oven just before bedtime on Thanksgiving eve and let it cook all night. I'll always remember the Thanksgiving many years later when I offered to cook the turkey. More of a canned cranberry sauce kind-of-a-girl, my extended family was taking a bit of a risk by entrusting me with the cooking and delivering of the main dish.

I woke up before daybreak that Thursday morning and put the turkey in the oven. I set my alarm for a few hours later, anticipating that aroma similar to what I had experienced growing up. However, when I awoke, my olfactory senses told me that something was seriously wrong. I went downstairs to discover the turkey patiently waiting in the oven for me to do something important in the cooking process—press the start button on my new digital oven. All I had done was create an environment just warm enough to dish up an eight-pound batch of salmonella with wings.

My family partly blamed themselves for their naivety; so, like my undercooked turkey, I didn't get a lot of heat. My sister came through with the ham that year, which we filled up on, along with extra helpings of stuffing and sweet potato casserole.

When I think about that very first Thanksgiving several hundred years ago, I'm reminded that it was a meal of gratitude following a year of immense suffering and loss. At some point, we all have a first Thanksgiving. It's that first time a parent or grandparent's chair is empty at the holiday table. It's the first Thanksgiving following a divorce or the death of a child. At a time set aside to give thanks for the abundance of what we have, we still can't help but notice what's missing or different.

A story that shows us God's heart towards us during these times is the story of Lazarus in John chapter 11. Lazarus and his sisters, Mary and Martha, were friends of Jesus. When Lazarus died, it was the first account we have of Jesus weeping. Even though He knew that He would raise

Lazarus back to life, He still cried when He saw the grieving family.

When our hearts are hurting, our Heavenly Father wants to remind us that He has a plan. His ways are not our ways and His timing may not always make sense. But no matter what is going on around us, we can trust in His faithfulness and unchanging love.

So, whether we prefer the Pilgrim variety with the buckle or a feathery Native American headdress, God's love and faithfulness are something we can always hang our hat on. And that, truly, is a reason to give thanks.

SNOW GLOBE

Snowfall in North Carolina is a big deal, especially in areas that typically don't see that much. For those of you who are unfamiliar with what happens in the South when this sort of thing takes place, allow me to give you a crash course in Southern Winter Weather Preparedness 101.

Winter precipitation is something we Southerners get really excited—or at least really worked up—about. All it takes is the mere mention of the "s" word in a weather forecast, and there is a rush on grocery stores much like that on the banks at the start of the Great Depression. Staple items such as bread, milk, and eggs begin flying off the shelves. At closing time, many of these stores resemble ancient Egypt just after the plague of locusts passed through.

Now, it is important to understand that we are not talking about forecasts predicting several feet or even several inches of snow. Just the threat of a dusting sends us Southerners into a frenzy.

Over the years, experts have tried to arrive at possible explanations for this irrational behavior. One theory is that since Southerners have less experience than our northern neighbors at dealing with the frozen stuff, we overcompensate. Another theory suggests that, similar to a dog circling his bed several times before lying down, this behavior has been passed down from our ancestors, and we really don't know why we still do it.

I've always loved to watch it snow and cross my fingers whenever there is the possibility of it in the forecast. I've also always been fond of snow globes. Even though we now have the fancy, battery-operated variety, I'm partial to the old-fashioned kind. I remember as a little girl enjoying the simple pleasure of shaking a snow globe and watching the snow gently fall on the picturesque winter scene contained therein.

Life is a lot like a snow globe. Just when you think things have settled into a routine, something happens that shakes everything up again. For instance, when my older daughter got married, she moved an hour away. I had just grown accustomed to the extra time tacked on to my drive to visit her when she and her husband moved out west for six months for his military training. Following that move, they relocated to Alaska. For a mom who cried for two weeks after her firstborn went off to college thirty minutes from home, it felt like she had moved to Mars.

Most of us, at one time or another, have wished that life could be like the scene in a snow globe when everything is calm and settled. We long for that safe, Christmas card-type image instead of the Weather Channel blizzard photos that life can also resemble. I think part of this longing is because we want the challenges we face to be manageable. We don't want to feel overwhelmed or out of control. But life's trials don't usually present themselves in the form of flurries, but rather as storms.

There are two accounts in the Bible of Jesus and his disciples dealing with storms. They are referenced in Matthew 8:23-27 and Matthew 14:22-31. The first is the familiar passage of Jesus being asleep in the boat when a storm arises. His disciples wake him up, and He calms the storm. The next account is when Jesus walks across the wind-swept waves and calls Peter out of the boat to join him.

In both cases, Jesus responded when He was asked to help. In the first, He stood in the middle of the boat and told the storm to leave. In the second, He stood in the middle of the water and told Peter to come.

We may not always understand why God takes away some trials and requires us to persevere through others. But we can trust that He knows when the snow globe needs to be stilled and when it needs to be shaken. With Him in the picture, there is beauty in both.

ALTERNATE ENDING

Bell-bottoms, The Brady Bunch, and aerosol hairspray so toxic it could blind you if you aimed in the wrong direction. Welcome to growing up in the '70s! The family station wagon was comparable in size to small mobile home, and Campbell's Soup required not one, but two cans of water to dilute. And then there was the music. Every generation thinks their music was the best. (The music of the '70s really was...just saying...) Regardless of which genre was your favorite back then, one group that was a household name was The Carpenters. Richard and Karen Carpenter took the music world by storm, mostly because of Karen's pitch-perfect voice. Richard was, and still is, an accomplished pianist and composer, but it was Karen's voice that the world fell in love with. In addition, their image and lyrics were notably wholesome, a welcomed departure from the drug-permeated and politically-charged music scene of the '60s.

On the surface, this brother and sister duo appeared to be living the American dream of success and stardom. But underneath, a dark storm brewed. Karen suffered from anorexia nervosa, a devastating disease that caused her untimely death at the age of thirty-two.

I remember that February morning when I read about her passing in the newspaper. At that time in 1983, I—and the rest of the world, for that matter—didn't understand eating disorders like we do today. With that in mind, I think about how lonely Karen's journey must have been. Having read her biography, I wish I could go back in time and somehow help this incredibly gifted, and yet hurting, young woman.

The idea of time travel has always fascinated me. In fact, there's an element of it in my first book, *The Gates Manor Band*. As I was completing the sequel, I was reminded that, as a writer, I get to decide the ending of my books. There is a character in the series that I created to be a total creep. I had originally planned an unpleasant fate for him in the second book, knowing that my readers would cheer! But I chose a different destiny for him, and, therefore, an alternate ending to the book.

We've all had things happen in the past that we wish we could change. Charles Dickens' famous story *A Christmas Carol* depicts Ebenezer Scrooge, a Grinch-like character who is allowed to see what his life would have been like if he had made different choices. What inspires Scrooge to change was not so much the opportunity he's afforded to go back in time, but the second chance he's given to go forward.

Each of us has the gift of today to make changes that could affect the outcome of our lives. If we don't like our current trajectory, now is the time to make adjustments that could give us an alternate—and better—ending.

For some, the events of the past weigh us down like heavy chains similar to those carried by Jacob Marley in the early chapters of *A Christmas Carol*. If that is your experience, then Christmas brings a message of hope for you.

In Luke 4:18-19, Jesus said, "The Spirit of the Lord is on me, because he has anointed me to proclaim good news to the poor. He has sent me to proclaim freedom for the prisoners and recovery of sight for the blind, to set the oppressed free, to proclaim the year of the Lord's favor."

For people who are suffering, good news is something that is longed for but often seems out of reach. In His great love for us, God reached down to us to provide hope and a better way. Salvation and a second chance were born in a manger. It was the greatest Christmas present ever given: God's gift of His Son.

Sometimes heartache and despair are easy to spot. Our church hosts an annual outreach event in southeast Raleigh where we provide a free meal, coats, and Christmas gifts for the poor and underprivileged of that area. The needs there are obvious. But what about someone like Karen Carpenter whose brokenness wasn't quite so apparent?

One of the characters in my book addresses this by stating that lost people don't always look lost. When announcing the birth of Jesus to the shepherds, the angel of the Lord said, "Fear not; for, behold, I bring you good tidings of great joy which shall be to all people. For unto you is born this day in the city of David a savior which is Christ the Lord."

The savior came for ALL people who would receive Him. He has a plan— a story to write—for each of us. If we give Him our past, present, and future, He can give us not just an alternate ending, but also a beautiful, new beginning.

THE BIRTHDAY GIFT

For all the moms out there reading this, you'll understand when I say that when my daughter turned twenty-seven, I felt like I should be turning twenty-seven. It's amazing how fast the years go by. I remember my twenty-seventh year, but not because anything significant happened. In fact, it stands out in my mind as a year where nothing significant seemed to be happening at all.

And that's why I wrote this as a birthday gift for my daughter.

My daughter was born just two weeks after Christmas. I was like Mary that year in that I was "great with child." It was a special time, and not just because my little girl was about to make her big debut. It was special because I felt like I had a little something in common with Mary. I was about to step into motherhood, just as she had done centuries earlier. I could relate to the excitement, the anticipation, and the wonder of it all.

However, the time leading up to motherhood had been difficult for me. My husband and I had spent three years trotting back and forth to the doctor trying to find out why we couldn't get pregnant. We were at a point in our lives where we were ready to carry out the Genesis mandate of being fruitful and multiplying. But fruitfulness just wasn't happening, at least not for us. It is important to note that everyone else we knew was getting pregnant. EVERYONE. Couples who weren't trying were getting pregnant, couples who didn't want to get pregnant, single people, pets, soap opera characters—you name it. Babies were popping into wombs everywhere, except for mine.

After three years of doctor visits and a collection of negative pregnancy tests resembling a large pile of bones, we discovered the problem. Modern medicine went to work, and six months later, two lines showed up on that final—and fateful—pregnancy test.

In the months that followed, I was sick—a lot. Morning sickness blurred into midday sickness and evening sickness. Finally, in my sixth month, the nausea began to taper off. While I didn't enjoy spending all that time with my head in a toilet, I really didn't mind. Let me be clear that it wasn't because I have a high tolerance for pain and suffering. (Case in point, it's rumored that my doctor retired from medicine shortly after my labor and delivery.) I didn't mind because I had been given a gift for three and a half years:

The gift of *not* getting pregnant.

Not having what we desire, and not having yet met our goals is an integral part of God's plan for our lives. We all have those days, months, and, yes, even years when fulfillment seems to be just out of reach. I would mark my twenty-seventh year as one where I had almost given up on what I had assumed would be the next step in my life. Infertility caught me off guard. It was something I never thought I'd have to deal with. But it was the *not* having that made me appreciate the *having* when the time was right. And I was willing to pay the price.

Conception and gestation take place in the hidden and secret place. So often, that's also the case when God is at work in our lives forming something beautiful. It's happening; we just can't see it yet. Just as nine months is necessary to bring forth life, the waiting we are required to do is not without purpose. Our Heavenly Father is at work shaping our hearts, our circumstances, our relationships, and everything that concerns us to accomplish His will in our lives.

> *"We can rejoice, too, when we run into problems and trials, for we know that they help us develop endurance. And endurance develops strength of character, and character strengthens our confident hope of salvation. And this hope will not lead to disappointment. For we know how dearly God loves us, because he has given us the Holy Spirit to fill our hearts with his love."*
>
> — ROMANS 5:3-5

My daughter's twenty-seventh birthday was the first that she was unable to spend with the family. She was making a sacrifice familiar to those who have family serving in the military. In addition to what she might have expected to arrive at her door that year, my main present for her was this devotional in her honor. This is fitting, as she was a birthday present for me. When I found out I was pregnant all those years ago and did the math, I realized that she was conceived on my twenty-eighth birthday.

The gift that keeps on giving? She certainly is. Perhaps that's one of the reasons we named her Hope.

BYE-BYE RED BIRD

With my daughter two weeks away from returning home from college for the summer, I decided to use her empty upstairs bedroom to do some writing. Her window overlooks the front yard where I had a view of our oak tree budding back to life. Out of the corner of my eye, I caught a glimpse of something red. I put my laptop aside to take in the beauty of a cardinal that had chosen a branch on our oak tree as a perch. I don't know if he found our tree particularly accommodating, or perhaps he was checking out a female nearby. But, for some reason, he lingered. I promptly texted my niece. I knew that she would understand how this bird had not only captured my attention, but also my heart.

At the age of ninety, my dad had a signature red cardigan sweater. It had been a Christmas gift from years earlier. He literally wore it until it had holes (large ones) around the elbows. In fact, my niece, who lives in Georgia, commented that it was hard to picture Grandpa not wearing that red sweater. It encapsulated her favorite memories of him. Eventually, my sister made the inevitable decision to "take it to her house to wash it" from which, of course, it never returned.

My dad was my hero. He was both a World War II veteran and possibly the kindest, most selfless person I have ever known. He lingered at my mom's side for the ten-year duration of her brave battle with Alzheimer's. While grieving her loss following sixty-two years of marriage, he lingered another two years after her passing. He lingered after two heart attacks, defying the odds, and returned from the hospital to live yet another two weeks. In his final moments, he was still determined to linger for as long as he could.

This bird, in his feathery red vest, made me think of my dad. It wasn't just in his taste for scarlet accessories, but in the way that he lingered.

My dad's lingering was an outward demonstration of an inward decision to not give up. He never gave up on the possibility of my mom getting better. He never gave up on his own health. In short, throwing in the towel was not an option for him.

The storms of life come to all of us. My dad was able to remain steadfast through his trials because he had an anchor for his soul. His hope, ultimately, was not in the temporal of this life, but in that which he knew to be eternal and unchanging.

The writer of the hymn penned it beautifully:

My hope is built on nothing less
Than Jesus blood and righteousness
I dare not trust the sweetest frame
But wholly lean on Jesus name.

My dad went to his heavenly home a few years ago on a November morning. In similar fashion, this cardinal, after lingering for another moment, flew away. It was a reminder to me of how short our time here on earth really is. Compared to eternity, it is much like this bird's brief perch on the branch of our oak tree.

For those of you curious about the fate of that red sweater...we secretly saved it (holes and all), and I found it while sorting through my dad's belongings. It migrated south to Atlanta last winter where my niece opened it, as a gift, on Christmas morning.

MERRY CHRISTMAS, CHARLIE BROWN

As the holiday season approaches, we're all visited by childhood memories of Christmas past. I'm thankful that mine are those of candlelight church services, home-cooked meals, and time with family. My parents didn't have the means to gratify every sugar plum vision that danced in our heads, but Christmas around our house was special all the same. Christmas and birthdays were the two occasions my parents designated for gift giving. Bonus rounds were Easter, where a candy-laden basket awaited us on Sunday morning, and Tooth Fairy visits, where net gains averaged around twenty-five cents per tooth.

One of my favorite Christmas memories was that of my dad arriving home with the family Christmas tree. We rarely purchased a tree, but more often made use of the few acres of farmland that my grandmother owned out in the country. Armed with a shovel, bucket, and a bundle of twine, my dad would dig up a tree, usually a cedar, and bring it home. We would cover the bucket with tin foil, decorate the tree, and my dad would plant it after the holidays. (He was eco-friendly decades before it was cool!)

I'll never forget the Christmas when he pulled into the driveway with what we dubbed the "Charlie Brown Christmas Tree." My siblings and I were self-proclaimed experts at determining if the evergreen houseguest he brought home each year was ornament-worthy. One look at this scrawny arrangement of branches in a bucket and our verdict was a unanimous, "No!"

But for some reason, a reason we wouldn't understand until years later, my dad liked this tree and insisted that we keep it. After Christmas, when our street was lined with discarded trees shedding needles and stray pieces of silver tinsel, he planted it. The humiliation we had experienced in the privacy of our home had moved outside to the front yard. As children with a sense of Christmas tree pride —and a cousin next door who was a bit competitive about such things—this public shame was almost more than we could bear.

Our fragile egos recovered, however, and the next year my dad redeemed himself and brought us home a proper tree. We almost forgot about the Charlie Brown Christmas Tree. And then, something akin to a Christmas miracle happened. That little cedar began to grow and take shape. A few years later, it had matured into a towering masterpiece that would rival any tree displayed in a store, much less in our cousin's living room. My dad adorned it with hundreds of lights and lit it every Christmas in the years that followed —forty to be exact. People from all over town came to see it. Finally, the Christmas after my mom died, my then eighty-nine-year-old dad decided it was time to pull the plug on the Charlie Brown Christmas Tree.

For those of us who grew up watching the Charlie Brown television specials, we're well acquainted with the title character who was consistently the underdog. He never got to kick the football and, on Halloween, he was the crestfallen trick-or-treater who went home with a bag full of rocks. At Christmas, he continued his legacy of never getting it right. When given the task of selecting a Christmas tree for the school play, he browsed through an impressive inventory of aluminum trees only to choose a small, spindly one that was ridiculed by his classmates.

My dad always had a place in his heart for the underdog. If he was watching sports on television and didn't have a favorite team, he would pull for the team that was losing. His compassion for those less fortunate was never more evident than around the holidays. Each year, he set out gifts by the roadside for the garbage collectors. One Christmas, he had us to gather the toys we weren't playing with anymore and he took them to a needy family. So when he, like Charlie Brown, was drawn to a little tree that would have been passed over by everyone else, we weren't all that surprised.

An Old Testament story that contains a hidden Christmas message is the account of Samuel the prophet anointing David as king. In 1 Samuel 16, God told Samuel that one of Jesse's sons was to be the next king of Israel. Saul, the current king, had failed as the leader of God's people. Though he was a head taller than everyone else, his heart wasn't right before God. David, on the other hand, was the runt of the litter whose job was to watch his father's sheep. Jesse had his older sons pass before Samuel, but Samuel declared that that none of them had been chosen. He had to ask Jesse if he had any other sons. Jesse was so sure that God wouldn't choose the youngest and the smallest, that he didn't even have David there for the lineup!

When David was presented, God spoke to Samuel and said, "He's the one."

God saw something in David that no one else could see. He saw his potential, and more importantly, He saw that David's heart was completely surrendered to Him.

At Christmas, if we only recognize Christ's coming without celebrating the manner in which He came, we miss something important. Jesus didn't arrive in strength and stature like David's older brothers, but in weakness and humility as a child. If we had seen Him as a Christmas tree in the forest, perhaps we would have passed Him by. Maybe that's why many of His own people did. They were expecting a warrior intent on defeating their enemies. Instead, they got a king intent on winning their hearts.

When life's disappointments leave us feeling misunderstood, overlooked, and left out, Christmas brings us good news. God sees our value, even if others don't seem to. The casual observer would have missed it that first Christmas. It would have been easy to take in the sights and sounds of that cold, dirty stable and conclude that Jesus was just an unfortunate baby whose parents couldn't provide better accommodations. Those who came to worship Him saw past all of that and saw something more: they saw God's chosen one, the King of Israel.

The Charlie Brown Christmas tree still stands in the front yard where my dad planted it all those years ago. Someone else owns the property now, so one day it may not be there anymore. But the lesson that it taught us will live on in our hearts forever.

And that, Charlie Brown, is what Christmas is all about.

LEAP YEAR

There have been years when Christmas in North Carolina felt more like spring break in the Bahamas. Instead of coming inside to warm our hands by the fire, we come inside to cool off from the heat and humidity. Hence the inspiration for my version of an old song:

Raindrops on roses
that shouldn't be blooming
Santa is sweating
And thunderstorms are looming
Brown UPS trucks
delivering bling
The calendar says it's Christmas
but it feels just like spring!
Cream-colored lattes that taste better cold now
We're pulling out lawn chairs
to rinse and unfold now
While others wear mittens
we're wearing sunscreen
The calendar says it's Christmas

but it feels just like spring!
When the kite flies
When the bee stings
You might think it's May
But here in the good old Tarheel State
We're just approaching Christmas Day!

Whether your Christmas is white or, like us North Carolinians, that white Christmas is experienced only in your dreams, the next holiday that we all look forward to is New Year's Eve.

New Year's Eve is sort of like the last course in a big winter meal. The main dish, and all the preparation that goes with it, is Christmas. New Year's is like coffee and dessert. It's the time where we can relax with friends and family and watch football, host a party, or do whatever it is we do to celebrate. It provides us with something we all want (and need) from time to time: a chance to start over. It's an opportunity to evaluate our lives and see where change is needed. And we have a fresh, new year to take steps to implement those changes.

Every four years we have the occurrence of a Leap Year. When that occurs, I want to challenge us to not just take steps, but to leap. Instead of making resolutions in an attempt to correct past errors, how about we instead focus on goals that cause us to move, or even leap, outside of what is comfortable and familiar?

We've all heard Bible stories about people who accomplished great things for God. We often think of them as super-humans, but they were just ordinary people like you and me. What set them apart was that they were willing to step out, take a risk, and obey God. After they did their part, they believed God to do only what He could do. Noah built a boat, but God brought the rain. Moses threw down the staff, but God turned it into a serpent.

Obeying God's calling on our lives is always going to require us to believe in things that are just beyond our reach and just outside of our human ability to make them happen. The Bible calls that faith. Paul defines faith in Hebrews 11:1. "Faith is the substance of things hoped for, the evidence of things not seen."

Maybe that's why it's called a "Leap of Faith." And every four years, we get an extra day to make that happen.

WELL DONE

There's just something about the sound of a mom's voice. It can be comforting and reassuring, or it can have the opposite effect, sending small animals scurrying into their burrows. It's critical that children and fathers alike learn what various pitches, tones, and volume levels mean. Here is a quick tutorial:

When a mom whispers:

This is a good thing when it's used to convey tender affection to a child who is drifting off to sleep after a bedtime story. However, if it's used in church and is accompanied by a stare that exposes all the capillaries in her eyes, it's at least a DEFCON 2 and the targeted offspring needs to cease and desist all questionable activity.

When a mom raises her voice:

The key here in determining threat level is context. For example, if a mom is shouting to be heard over a loud television or her son practicing the drums, there is no cause for alarm. But if this increase in volume is the result of her finding a young one playing with matches or eating the dessert meant for the PTA meeting, it should be taken seriously.

When a mom speaks in low tones:

A mom's last resort. This is a cue that she means business, especially when its used in public or over the phone. *"You leave that party right now, or I will drive over and bring you home myself."* A mom lowering her voice is trying to do her job without causing a scene.

My mom employed all of the above at one time or another. One of the occasions she regularly raised her voice —and we knew not to be concerned—was when she called us to dinner. In fact, it wasn't just that no one was concerned; it was as if no one heard her at all. She would have to call several times before family members even began looking in the direction of the kitchen.

I thought perhaps this was just a quirk with my family until I became a mom myself. Then I learned that there's something about saying "dinner's ready" that renders all within earshot hearing impaired.

In terms of what was served once everyone (finally) took their seat at the table, my mom was an old-fashioned Southern cook. During the week, meals were heavy on the side of vegetables and homemade biscuits. Meat or poultry was reserved for the weekends, where the line-up was typically steak on Thursday night, fish on Friday, and a nice roast for Sunday lunch.

When it came to how beef was prepared, both of my parents had a fear of the undercooked. If pink was found in your meat, it meant certain death. I didn't have a steak that was cooked medium until I was twelve years old. I was at my friend Polly's house, and her dad was cooking them on the grill. I had never tasted meat that still had juice in it. It was great!

While well-done is used to describe meat that has been

fully cooked, it's also an expression used to praise someone who's completed an assignment with skill and proficiency. (Note: A mom's well done is said in a happy tone and is often followed by a hug.)

We all need to hear a "well done" from time to time. The most important time will be when this life is over and we're standing before our Heavenly Father.

Many of us are familiar with the parable of the talents. In Matthew 25:14-30, Jesus tells the story of a man who went away on a long journey. While he was gone, he entrusted the oversight of his assets to his three servants. One was wicked and buried the talents he was given to manage instead of investing them. The other two invested theirs and received a handsome return on their money. They were the ones who, when the master returned, were told, "Well done, my good and faithful servants."

It's interesting that all three servants were given the same opportunity for success. Evidently, all were competent, or they wouldn't have had a job. But there was something hidden and undealt with in the character of the wicked servant that prevented him from successfully completing his assignment.

In His great love for us, our Heavenly Father allows situations to come into our lives to deal with such issues. Much like that well-done steak, the heat from these fiery trials penetrates through the layers of our heart, making sure no area is left untouched. If we embrace these processes, even though they can be difficult to endure, we come out on the other side better equipped to fulfill our God-given destiny.

A well-done steak is one that has stayed in the heat a little longer than the others. When trials seem to go on forever, Scripture encourages us to not lose heart but to remember that these difficult seasons serve to mature us in the faith. We read in James 1:2-4: "Consider it pure joy, my brothers and sisters, whenever you face trials of many kinds, because you know that the testing of your faith produces perseverance. Let perseverance finish its work so that you may be mature and complete, not lacking anything."

We all experience trials that purify us and build endurance. We also enjoy seasons of blue skies, belly laughs, and days where everything seems to fall into place. Our Heavenly Father knows what we need in order for the likeness of His Son to be formed in our lives. In the middle of it all, He's blessed us with His creation to enjoy, people to love, and stories to write. We're so underserving of this amazing grace.

With this in mind, at the end of the day, and at the end of our journey, we can look to the heavens, smile, and say,

"Well done!"

ROCKIN' ROBIN

Not long ago, I found a cassette tape collection that belonged to my parents. It's something I run across from time to time when I'm rummaging through the family museum that is my attic looking for something. This time, out of curiosity, I paused to read the label on each one to see which was the oldest. The winner? Christmas morning, 1976. I decided to listen to it. When I did, it was like stepping into a time machine. In addition to the sound of wrapping paper being torn off gifts, I could hear my family talking, laughing, and enjoying the holiday together.

One conversation, in particular, caught my attention. It was between my dad and me. Evidently, I had given him a toboggan that year. He was grateful for it and responded like I had just handed him the keys to a new car instead of an inexpensive, dime store hat. Just before he opened it, he read aloud the tag "From Jan to Daddy." Then he chuckled.

My dad was a hard worker who made sure I had food to eat, a roof over my head, clothes on my back, an education, and all the other things that parents provide. He probably even provided me with the money I needed for my

Christmas shopping that year. I could never in a lifetime have given him anything that would come close to evening the score. Maybe he knew that. Maybe that's why he chuckled.

That's how I feel as I dedicate this devotion to a lady whose writing has deeply inspired and motivated me. I've walked through some difficult trials, but nothing like what she and her family have faced. I feel like I'm giving her a dime store hat when she's given me the keys to a new car.

Her name is Elizabeth, and her husband, Robin, passed away from ALS at the young age of fifty-one. Elizabeth documented Robin's journey on social media to keep everyone updated on his condition. In doing so, she didn't sugarcoat the situation but was candid about what it's like to watch someone you love fight for his life.

I was impressed with Elizabeth's posts because, as Christians, we're often afraid to admit there are things in life that we don't have answers for. We're reluctant to disclose just how bloody the battle really is. But in doing so, we diminish the significance of the victory.

Trials aren't something that Jesus said *might* happen. Rather, he guaranteed that they would. In the familiar parable of the two houses—one built on sand and one built on rock—the storm came to both houses. Trials affect everyone, Christians and non-Christians alike.

But here's the difference:

The house built on the sand depends on our ability to save ourselves, or anything other than eternal Truth. That may be sufficient for fair weather. It may even survive a small gale or two. But when the real storms of life hit, this house begins sinking in the shifting sand of human emotion. Its occupants quickly learn that people will fail and disappoint us. What we thought was unshakable is proven to be temporary and unreliable.

The house that is built on Christ is set on a firm foundation that will stand regardless of what life brings. This Truth is not just a belief system, but the person of Jesus. When the waters rise, His glorious presence is with us, reassuring us that we don't have to be afraid.

Robin experienced Christ's presence in the middle of his storm. He had a smile when the pain was overwhelming, and a positive word even when the disease impeded his speech. He knew Jesus as both savior and master builder. He understood that a place for him in heaven was under construction where he would no longer suffer from ALS. But while he was still here, and the storm huffed and puffed, his house stood strong.

Over time, Robin acquired a nickname. While this term of endearment paid tribute to his determination and optimism, I think it also spoke of the solid rock on which he stood.

Yes, Rockin' Robin certainly did suit him.

BACKING UP

By the time you've reached my age, you've been around the block a few times. (Okay, let's get real here. It's more like circling the globe.) But to get into a car accident, I never had to travel very far.

Let me explain.

Many years ago (on Thanksgiving, no less), I managed to run into my husband's car while backing out of the driveway. Fast-forward about eight years, and there I was, sideswiping his SUV while—you guessed it—backing out of the driveway. But it doesn't end there. Later, I hit my own car while backing out with his. And then, when my oldest daughter got her first car, I backed into it. Evidently, my mindset was that you don't have to leave your own driveway to damage another vehicle. No need to waste all that gas by pulling out onto the street.

While my obvious disregard for a rear-view mirror has resulted in unsightly dents and higher insurance premiums, putting the car in reverse doesn't have to be problematic. In fact, going backwards can be a positive thing.

For example, I've watched each of my daughters back out

of the driveway en route to various milestones and rites of passage: a first date, the first day of high school, senior prom, the first time they returned to college after a weekend home, or the first time they left for the airport on their own.

When we think of backing up, we often think of losing ground. But in Scripture, it can be the biggest step in moving forward.

There's an aspect to the Christian life that's just as important as gas and oil in a car. Without it, we find ourselves burning out or spinning our wheels. Perhaps we don't have the joy we once had. We may be attending Bible study, church, and even serving those in the community. Yet, something is still missing.

In Revelation 2:2-5, we read about the church at Ephesus who, from all outward appearances, was doing the right things. While Christ acknowledges the people's good deeds, he admonishes them regarding an unseen—and more significant—issue.

He says, "I know your deeds and your toil and perseverance, and that you cannot tolerate evil men, and you put to the test those who call themselves apostles, and they are not, and you found them to be false; and you have perseverance and have endured for My name's sake, and have not grown weary. But I have this against you, that you have left your first love. Therefore, remember from where you have fallen, and repent and do the deeds you did at first..."

Where this church—like so many of us—got off track was by leaving their first love. Without that vibrant, first-love relationship with Christ burning inside our hearts, we become like any other group or organization that maintains certain disciplines and engages in humanitarian efforts. (You don't have to be a Christian to visit someone in prison or volunteer at a soup kitchen.) In order to reclaim that relationship, we have to go back. Back to what we did when we first fell in love with Him. Back to when we couldn't wait to read Scripture or spend time in prayer. Going back and doing what we did at first propels us forward with a renewed sense of strength and purpose.

Another example in Scripture of works versus relationship is Mary and Martha. While Martha busied herself in the kitchen preparing a meal, Mary chose to sit at the feet of Jesus. The lesson in the story is that service is important, but not on an empty tank.

When we have opportunity to do good for those around us, let us first take time with the Savior. Before we serve a meal to someone who is less fortunate, let us feast on His word. Then, we won't just be meeting a temporary need; we'll be offering the eternal Bread of Life.

Even though my driving record has improved over the years, family members still cringe when they have the unfortunate fate of parking behind me. I guess it really is important to use that rear view mirror. Going forward, I'll have to make sure that I do.

FINISH LINE

I'll always remember when my oldest daughter participated in her first elementary school Field Day. Her teacher had signed her up for the marble spoon race. She awoke early that spring morning ready to take on the world, or at least the other kindergarteners who were competing for those coveted blue ribbons.

When her event began, I had my camera strategically positioned to capture the Kodak moment of her victoriously crossing the finish line. Unfortunately, she only got a few steps down the field when that marble rolled off her spoon and landed in the dirt. I can still see the swish of her blonde ponytail as she spun around to look at me. Her expression was one of disbelief and heartbreak. Needless to say, the next year we took on the marble spoon race as if it were an Olympic event. And somewhere in our attic is her second place ribbon. The following year, she won first.

With sporting events, there's always a finish line or a goal. And it's different with every sport. With football, it's running the ball into the end zone. Basketball courts have the two opposing hoops. With soccer, it's kicking the ball past the goalie and into the net. But all of these sports have one thing in common: a clock.

Time is a tricky thing. When you're young, it seems to crawl; especially when you're waiting for your birthday or Christmas to arrive. As you get older, Father Time begins to move along at a much faster clip. Each year when the holidays arrive, I feel like I just put my decorations away from last year.

I had a favorite uncle who passed away unexpectedly a few years ago. He was a "salt of the earth" kind of guy, with a calm, quiet strength. He was a devoted family man and an honest hard worker who was always willing to help someone in need.

With his passing, I was reminded that life has a finish line. The only difference is that, unlike sporting events, we don't get to see the clock ticking down. When a running back knows there are only seconds on the clock, he is going to make sure that he makes the most of the time to score a touchdown. In life, we don't have that luxury.

But that's a good thing.

There is a familiar passage in John chapter 14 that is often read at funerals. Jesus said, "In my father's house are many mansions. If it were not so, I would have told you. I go to prepare a place for you. And if I go and prepare a place for you, I will come again and receive you unto myself; that where I am, there you may be also."

Jesus was referring to a Jewish wedding custom of the day. After a young man received a "yes" from his prospective bride, he would go away for a period of time to build a house for them. When everything was ready, he would come back for her. Not knowing when her groom would be returning, the bride couldn't afford to get lazy or distracted. She had to be ready at all times.

This is a beautiful depiction of how the Gospel is a love

story. Jesus refers to the Church as His bride. And not knowing when He will be returning means we need to keep our love for Him fresh and our hope alive. It's designed to keep us from getting lazy or distracted. We need to be ready at all times.

My daughter's blue ribbon has probably faded by now. It was only a marble spoon race, but it was an early life lesson on how to finish strong. When my uncle crossed his finish line, he entered heaven, not because of an attic full of blue ribbons based on his own merit, but because he had said yes to Jesus. He will receive an eternal inheritance that will never perish, spoil, or fade. It's based on the ultimate victory that Jesus won on our behalf on the cross. And one day, I will see him again.

Final score: Jesus–1 Death–0

ABOUT THE AUTHOR

Jan Hemby is a native North Carolinian who is proud of her small town heritage. The goal of her writing is to bring the truth of God's love to everyday life through messages that are fresh and relevant. Her first novel, *The Gates Manor Band,* was released in 2016. The sequel, *Secrets and Surrender,* will be published in 2018.

Jan currently lives in North Carolina with her husband of thirty years, Billy. They have two grown daughters, Hope and Cara, and two grand-puppies, Gatsby and Daisy.

Find Jan on the web at
www.janhemby.com/